A SCORE SETTLED!
Part Two

By Kim Hunter

Dedication

For my dear friend Marge.
Gone but never forgotten.

1952 – 2018

INDEX

Chapter twenty-three
Chapter twenty-four

Kim Hunter

Copyright © 2018 by Kim Hunter

OTHER WORKS BY KIM HUNTER

Web site **www.kimhunterauthor.com**

ACKNOWLEDGEMENT

Thanks to Kevin Plume for all of your help.

To life for giving me this opportunity.

Heartfelt thanks to each and every one of you
who purchase my work and allow me the
opportunity to do what I love.

FOREWORD

Life asked death, "Why do people love me but hate you?" Death responded, "Because you are a beautiful lie and I am a painful truth."

—Author unknown

"What greater thing is there for two human souls, than to feel that they are joined for life to strengthen each other in all labour, to rest on each other in all sorrow, to minister to each other in all pain, to be one with each other in silent unspeakable memories at the moment of the last parting?"

— **George Eliot, Adam Bede**

PROLOGUE

Through no fault of her own, Shauna O'Malley had suffered a life of total and utter neglect. Abused beyond belief though absolutely nothing she'd been forced to endure could ever have prepared her for losing her mother Violet and baby sister Vonny. Dragged up in a squalid excuse for a flat the two small children had not only been witness to Violet's prostitution but also suffered regular beatings by the drunken Irishwoman they had the sad misfortune to call Mum. At a mere nine years old Shauna's role was that of both mother and housemaid to the two females in her life and although for entirely different reasons, she knew that neither could survive without her. Life was shit for the little girl but it became even tougher when a certain young, aspiring gangster suddenly appeared in their lives.

From the onset Shauna had hated Davey Wiseman but she didn't have a say in her mother's love life and the term 'love' could only be used loosely. Violet O'Malley fell for the up and coming gangster in a big way but Davey hadn't been privy to the fact that his new woman was also a brass. When he found out, things were about to change and it was now payback time! Slowly he intentionally introduced Violet to the highs of heroin and when she was well and truly hooked he walked away but not before supplying her with one last fatal dose. That night as Violet lay dying Vonny had quietly crept into the room and after playing with the syringe, decided in her innocence to be a big girl by sticking the needle into her arm just like mummy always did. The tube only contained a small amount of the drug but it was more than enough and the innocent child was dead within a matter of minutes.

After the deaths Shauna had been placed into the hands of Sunrise Care Home where she would remain until adulthood. A few days after she arrived she had bonded with a lady named Jackie Silver, both the girl and her carer had somehow never fitted into any of society's boxes that others seemed to happily adhere to. Nonetheless they had been drawn to each other and Jackie or 'Jacks' as Shauna always referred to her, soon became a surrogate mother. Shauna had never talked about her family or what had happened back in that East London flat but Jackie quickly realised that it must have been pretty horrific. She would often hear Shauna talking to someone when the
little girl was alone and thought that no one could hear her. It turned out to be her dead sister Vonny and for a while Jackie worried that Shauna might need psychiatric help. She didn't, she was just a small child that simply missed her sister so badly that she imagined she could talk to her and it seemed she could because Shauna O'Malley would always hear Vonny's advice as clearly as if her baby sister had actually been in the room with her. . No family had ever wanted to foster her, well at least not after having her in their own homes for a few hours. Shauna would misbehave and do anything she could to cause a ruckus or upset people until she was returned to the only place she felt safe, 'Sunrise'.

At eighteen and as the law states, Shauna was forced to leave Sunrise but not before Jackie had already secured her accommodation in a shared house and employment at a factory close by to the property. It wasn't what she had wanted for her young friend but Shauna never once complained, in fact she knuckled down and was an ideal employee. The two would religiously meet every Sunday for lunch and once a year they would take a holiday and spend a complete week together. Over the next ten or so years their closeness never faltered but at the end of yet another fabulous holiday in Bournemouth, which once again had been nothing but fun and total relaxation, all was about to change forever. Never in her worst nightmares did Jackie expect the explosive bombshell Shauna was about to drop. What scared Jackie further was that the revelation had been revealed in such a matter of fact manner, as if it was the most natural thing in the world to occur. She had a plan, a plan that had been years in the making, she was going after Davey Wiseman! Jackie desperately tried to talk her out of such a ludicrous idea, but when Shauna made her mind up over something, a fact Jackie had come to learn very early on, then there was absolutely no stopping her and this time she was hell bent on making him pay for what he'd done.

Nearly twelve months on and it was all systems go but on the day Shauna eventually departed for London she gave Jackie no warning whatsoever. A simple envelope was propped up on the mantel piece, a sad little note containing the only information she was willing to share with her one true friend, a friend who absolutely adored her and in fact was the only person in the entire world who gave a damn whether she lived or died.

Arriving in London Shauna completely changed her appearance, her long ebony hair was cut into a bob and dyed the colour of copper and her youthful clothes were swapped for clean lined, classy items. Shauna O'Malley now went by the name of Frances Richards and to anyone that may have known Violet years earlier, upon seeing

Shauna would have thought it was the dead woman reincarnated. That was exactly what Shauna had planned and she was so determined to be the double of her mother that she even started to wear the same perfume. Locating Davey Wiseman wasn't too much of a problem but getting into a situation where she could meet him face to face was an entirely different matter. Eventually Shauna found a job at a small newsagent, several months later and purely by luck, she suddenly and unexpectedly came face to face with the man who had cruelly torn her family apart.

Davey was very taken with the young woman's appearance, so much so in fact, that within a few days he had invited her out to dinner. There began Shauna's mission to make him fall for her so deeply that she would be able to gain access into his inner circle and hopefully obtain crucial information that would put him where he belonged, behind bars for the rest of his life. What Shauna hadn't bargained on was the undying loyalty of his lifelong friend Billy Jackson. Billy was one of the toughest, meanest bastards in London but he was also outwardly gay and insanely in love with his best friend. His jealousy was so great that when Davey first introduced him to Shauna or Fran as he knew her, he had instantly taken a dislike to the woman and decided there and then that she had to go and go quickly. The man's loathing of her was so intense that it rapidly forced a wedge between him and Davey, a wedge that would cause immense heartbreak for Billy and eventually force him to physically threaten Shauna's life.

Gilly Slade worked as a right hand man for Davey and the instant he set eyes on Shauna he fell head over heels in love with her but the feeling wasn't in any way mutual.

Still, she did her utmost to encourage a friendship with Gilly without in any way leading him on, in the vain hope that he would reveal something to her, anything that would enable her to get revenge for all that Davey had put her through. Shauna strangely enjoyed all the attention of being courted, the wining and the dining, even the sex but what she hadn't bargained on was falling in love with the enemy. Still her mind was made up and she would allow absolutely nothing to get in her way. When months later she learned of a major drug deal that was about to take place involving Billy and Davey, Shauna sought out the help of D.I. Neil Maddock. For years the detective had been trying to nail Davey Wiseman and put him behind bars but as grateful as he was for the information, he showed Shauna little loyalty after the arrests. In one particular interview the man had actually gloated to Davey regarding who had grassed him up, that revelation would undoubtedly seal Shauna O'Malley's fate.

Gilly, along with others who would hunt down anyone for a price, were dispatched to find her, luckily he located Shauna first and managed to swiftly get her out of London. Soon after returning to the holiday cottage in Bournemouth and the safety of being with Jackie, Shauna discovered she was pregnant with Davey's baby. It was a shock but one she quickly came to terms with and the idea of the impending child soon had her and Jackie in a nervous but excited state.

The high profile case came to court three months later and when Davey was sentenced to fifteen years the anti was upped and a price of two hundred thousand pounds was placed on Shauna's head. Unsure as to where she was staying Gilly was frantic with worry and when he did manage to make contact, he urgently warned her that she had to go into hiding, disappear in fact. He then suddenly and out of the blue asked her to go away with him. Gilly had booked two tickets to Florida leaving the very next day. He was gentle in his approach and didn't try to force her but she had instantly dismissed the idea out of hand. After discussing the grave situation further she finally realised that by staying she would be putting not only her own and Jackie's lives at risk but also that of her unborn child, Shauna decided to take up his offer. Sadly things didn't work out as planned.

Around this time new corrupt and indisputable evidence had come to light. A certain Met Superintendent, James Loftwood, had previously been a frequent visitor to one of Davey's most debauched clubs 'The Judge's Den'. He'd had a liking for young girls, the younger the better in fact and would carry out his sickening, depraved and sadistic sexual fantasies without any concerns whatsoever for the emotional state of the children involved. As soon as Davey had been sentenced, James was anonymously tipped off that his deviant acts had been recorded by hidden cameras. Fear of the images ever seeing the light of day, along with the threat of prosecution saw him take his own life but not before he had made his own recording stating that he had been party to a corrupt set up by The Met to incarcerate Davey Wiseman. This was of course complete and utter nonsense but James Loftwood had made the statement in the hope that it would gain Davey his freedom and stop the gangster from ever releasing the sick footage, footage that James knew would undoubtedly break the hearts of his already devastated wife and children.

Shauna waited for Jackie to leave the house and after once again placing a note on the mantel piece, she climbed into what she thought was her pre-ordered taxi. Unbeknown to her, they had somehow found out her whereabouts and the driver was no cabbie but actually one of Davey's men. The vehicle hadn't travelled more than a couple of miles when it suddenly dawned on Shauna what was actually happening. Even though the car was in motion she attempted to get out but quickly discovered that the rear doors were locked. With no possible means of escape, all she could do was try and desperately plead for her life and that of her unborn child but it was all to no avail and her cries fell on deaf ears. Within hours Shauna O'Malley had become a prisoner, incarcerated in a dark and dank basement with no means of escape.

CHAPTER ONE

Shauna woke with a start and it took a moment for her eyes to fully focus and for her to remember where she now was. The bare bulb had been burning all night and for the first few hours its orange glow had stopped her from sleeping. There was no way to turn it off and she wondered if this had been done on purpose as a kind of torture. Trying to stand up from the low camp bed was difficult and it took several attempts before she was finally on her feet. Vigorously rubbing at her back which ached like hell she suddenly felt her baby move and for just a fleeting moment as she stroked her ever expanding stomach, she smiled. Baby suddenly became still and once more she was alert to her surroundings. A small torch had been placed onto the upturned beer crate that now acted as a makeshift table and reaching down she switched it on and shone its beam into the dark corners of the room. Slowly hobbling around she hoped to see something, a boarded up window, anything that just might give her a means of escape but there was nothing. The musty smell of damp was nauseating and glancing down she knew it was coming from the bare earth that she was standing on but she wouldn't allow herself to be beaten, she'd come too far and suffered too much to give in now. Davey might have won the battle but the war was far from over and while she still had a breath in her body she would fight for the life growing inside of her. Hearing the door being unlocked she backed into the corner and switched off the torch. Ray Harvey had been told by Barry McCann to take food over to the house. He had also been instructed to make no conversation whatsoever with the woman there but as much as Ray feared the man he worked for, he wasn't uncompassionate, a rare thing in their line of work. Closing the basement door behind him he slowly descended the rickety wooden stairs and for a moment thought that she'd escaped but Shauna was breathing so hard and the room was so cold that he glimpsed the breath as it escaped her lips.

"You can come out, I won't hurt you."

Sobbing gently, Shauna slowly stepped forward, her face was tearstained and dirty and when Ray saw her condition he was shocked to the core. Glancing round his eyes fell upon a dilapidated armchair and dragging it into the centre of the room he beckoned for her to sit. Shauna's back was killing her and knowing there was no way out, at least for the moment, she did as she was asked.

"There, that's better isn't it?"

Shauna gently nodded her head, the fabric was damp and the springs in the seat had gone in places but it was still better than having to lie on the camp bed for hours. Ray handed over a carrier bag which held sandwiches and a flask of coffee. Even though she was starving, Shauna instantly opened the thermos and poured herself a hot drink. After taking a mouthful she sighed heavily.

"How long will I be here?"

Ray was reluctant to engage, he'd been warned what would happen but his heart went out to the young woman. He hadn't got a clue what on earth his boss was up to but Ray didn't like it one bit. They might be gangsters dealing out violence as and when it was called for but kidnapping women? Really? That was a definite no no in his book, Barry had crossed a line and now Ray really didn't want to be involved. "I honestly don't know

love, I don't even know why you're here. I was only told
to bring food so that's what I've done."

"You could let me go?"

"Fuck me sweetheart that would be more than my life's
worth!"

"I wouldn't tell anyone, honest I wouldn't."

Glancing down he studied her vast stomach and then
looking into her tear stained face he smiled at her but it
was a sad kind of smile.

"I have kids of my own sweetheart and just like the
feeling you have for your baby, to me their safety is
paramount and at the end of the day they are all that
matter to me. Barry's a right nasty cunt and if I let you
out then me and mine would never be able to feel safe
again."

"What would they think of this, of you hurting me?"

Ray exhaled deeply, no way had he signed up for this and
the next time he saw his boss he was going to let Barry
have it with both fucking barrels. They did a lot of
things, things he wasn't proud of but this, holding a
pregnant woman hostage? It made him feel ashamed to
be associated with these men.

"I ain't hurting you sweetheart but I can't let you go
either. Now I don't know what you've done or who
you've pissed off to end up in this predicament but..."

"Davey Wiseman, that's who."

Ray gulped hard at the mention of the man's name. He
knew his boss did business with the very serious players
but Wiseman, well he was in another league altogether.

Shauna could feel the onset of tears again and they
weren't released to make the man feel pity but purely in
frustration and fear at the situation. Nodding her head
she wiped her eyes with the palm of her filthy hand and

then through bloodshot eyes gazed up into the man's face.

"I understand but my baby is only days away, it's my first and I don't know what to do. What if I go into labour?" Nodding, Ray smiled his understanding.

"Leave it with me love, I can't set you free but I can make things as comfortable as I can for you. Now I'm going to pop out for a bit but I'll be back as soon as I can, I promise."

Shauna lent her head back against the chair and closed her eyes. Seconds later she heard the door being locked and bolted, once again her tomb was sealed and fear started to take over as she tried to imagine where this was all going to end. Strangely since she'd been brought to this place she hadn't heard a peep from Vonny. It was as if her mind had now moved on from that part of her life and she no longer needed her little sister to egg her on.

Some two hours later, though having no way of telling the time to Shauna it felt like far longer, the basement door once again creaked open. This time Ray Harvey was carrying a large box and placing it onto the ground in front of her feet he opened it up and started to unpack the contents. She watched him but never said a word while all the time wondering if he would cave in and eventually set her free. It was a slim chance but she had to have something to cling onto, something that gave her hope that this wasn't where she would end her days.

"Now let's see! Right, I got towels, baby blankets and food, milk powder, scissors, oh and this."

Ray handed Shauna a thick book and when she saw the title 'How to Give Birth Alone' she wanted to scream out

4

in fear. So even when the baby came they weren't planning on helping her! What if things went wrong and she needed medical help? She could die or worse her baby could die!

"Oh no pleeeeeease!!!!!! I can't do this all alone, I don't know how!"

Standing up the man, this hard man who had in the past had a hand in many a brutal beating, now felt useless and if he was honest, he felt frightened for the young woman. Recalling the birth of his third child, when his wife Sally had haemorrhaged badly and it had been touch and go if she survived, he knew exactly what the young woman's fears were.

"I told you sweetheart, there's nothing I can do. I have to go now so please don't make things difficult for me."

"Difficult for you? Fuck you!!!!!"

Shauna's words had come out with such venom that Ray suddenly wondered if she was as innocent as she had first made out. Whether she was or she wasn't was irrelevant, his hands were tied and that was the end of it.

"I'll try and get back here this week but it will depend on what the boss has lined up for me. You might get Igors Petrov and if you do then take my advice do exactly what he tells you and don't dream of bad mouthing off to him. Igors is a complete cunt and always will be, hurting you wouldn't bother him in the slightest. It might sound a bit stupid but take care of yourself love and try not to worry."

Ray Harvey turned on his feet and within seconds had disappeared through the door. He couldn't wait to get out of the place and breathe fresh air again. He had hoped to return but now he willed Barry to send him back just so that he could keep an eye on the poor little cow.

Shauna was exhausted and standing up she then waddled over to the camp bed and gingerly lowered herself down onto the lumpy mattress. Lying on her side she faced the wall in an attempt to block out the glare from the light bulb and somehow she managed to drift off and it was several hours before she woke again. The rustling sound of the carrier bag disturbed her sleep and as she turned and looked towards the table, Shauna saw the biggest rat she had ever seen staring right back at her. Swallowing hard she tried to keep calm as she struggled to her feet. Her movement scared the animal and it quickly scurried away but not before it had taken a bite of the sandwich, the only food Shauna had until God knows when. Shining the torch onto an overhead beam she noticed a piece of string hanging down that must have been there for years. A gentle tug showed it was still capable of taking some weight so tying the carrier bag to it would at least ensure that her food would be safe if her only companion decided to return for a second sitting.

On her first day of incarceration the need to relieve herself had brought on a new challenge when Shauna realised that the only toilet facility was an old china chamber pot placed on a stool at the side of the staircase. It wasn't rocket science to work out that after a few toilet trips it wouldn't take long for her living quarters to start smelling and she tried to figure out a way of getting rid of her waste but there was nothing she could think of so her only option was to empty it on the ground in the corner of the room. By the time Ray had started to visit the basement was rank, flies were continually circling and each time the pot began to fill Shauna would place her cardigan over it in a vain attempt to lessen the stench.

The birthing book that the man had given her was a hardback and she decided that she could afford to lose the cover if nothing else. For over twenty minutes she had worked on the book wriggling the front from side to side until eventually it gave up the ghost and broke free. Walking over to the corner of the room she gently lowered herself down onto her knees and began to use the stiff cover to dig away at the soil. Shauna knew it had to be a sizeable hole as she didn't know how long she would need to use it. The sweat drenched her already dust covered body but she didn't stop until the task was finished and she at least had some kind of makeshift toilet at her disposal. Over the next few hours every time she wanted to pee she would carefully pour the contents of the chamber pot into the hole and then throw a little soil over to try and mask the smell. It worked to a degree but she seemed to be constantly going as the baby pressed on her bladder.

Luckily, the following morning Ray was once again her jailer and Shauna breathed a huge sigh of relief when she saw him descend the stair case. Throughout the night her imagination had run wild and grotesque visions of what this man Igors might have looked like had invaded her dreams. Shauna somehow managed a weak smile as she attempted to get up from the bed, she felt like a beached whale and Ray Harvey couldn't help but smile as he helped her to her feet.

"How are you feeling today?"

"Fat and useless to name but a few."

Ray laughed and Shauna smiled, maybe he was softening towards her. All she had to do was be nice and you never knew, he might be her knight in shining armour after all.

"I remember Sally, that's my wife by the way, she used to say very similar things when she was up the duff." Shauna found his turn of words distasteful but she didn't let him see and instead she waddled over to the old armchair and plonked herself down heavily onto the seat. "So how many children do you? By the way, my name's Shauna."

Ray didn't respond as he knew what she was doing, Barry had warned him that she was as crafty as a fox. The previous night he had driven the ninety four mile return trip to London and sought out his boss in an attempt to find out what the hell was going on and to say he was shocked by the conversation he'd had with Barry McCann was an understatement. His boss always hung out in The Ace of Spades Club on Sandal Road over in Edmonton. It may have been called a club but in all honesty it could only marginally pass as a pub and not a very good one at that. The Ace, as everyone referred to it, was an old school villain's establishment and you didn't enter unless you were of the same fraternity or very, very stupid. Deals were carried out there and jobs planned and if your face wasn't known you stuck out like a sore thumb.

Barry McCann was seated on his regular stool at the bar and when Ray entered and walked over his boss studied his face for any recognition that he'd gone soft. Had that have been the case then the man would have crawled out of the building and that would only have been if luck was on his side.

"How'd it go?"

Ray puffed out his cheeks as he slowly shook his head from side to side. The landlord knew the man's drink of

choice and it was poured and on the bar without Ray
having to ask.

"Okay but what the fuck is going on? She said Davey
Wiseman is involved."

"I thought I gave you strict fucking instructions not to
talk to her?"

"You might have guvnor but the same can't be said about
what comes out of her mouth now can it?"

"Tell me about it, right fucking lippy bitch she is. Look,
all I know is that she's the reason why Davey is doing
time. Now I took this job on because the pay is good
with no questions asked and I suggest you do the same.
Believe you me, you don't want to be answering to that
man, he's a right evil cunt. Now do what I pay you to
fucking do and no more questions. Go back tomorrow,
after that Igors can do it for a couple of days, I don't want
either of you getting too familiar with her, though if Igors
got familiar I don't think she'd know what had fucking
hit her."

The conversation ended there and after Ray had swiftly
downed his drink he left The Ace with a heavy heart.
Now here he was again and he still felt shit about the
whole fucking thing.

"Look Lady, this is all too fucking deep for me to get
mixed up in and I'd rather not talk to you. As from
tomorrow Big Igors will be coming here, now here's your
food for the day so make it last."

Shauna snatched the bag from his hand and peered inside.
It was sandwiches again and her body was crying out for
a hot meal and some proper nourishment but she knew
deep down that it wasn't going to happen. Ray walked
towards the stairs but stopped before he took his first
step.

"Remember what I told you, for your own sake don't give Igors any lip. I don't know if I'll be back again so believe me when I say I wish you all the fucking luck in the world as I think you're going to need it."
With that he was gone and Shauna couldn't hold back the tears as they came thick and fast.

CHAPTER TWO

In the days that had followed the deathbed confession of Superintendent James Loftwood, Davey had been busy, very busy in fact. When the news broke he had been catapulted to prison hero within the walls of Wormwood Scrubs. Everywhere he went he was patted on the back and words of congratulations were given in abundance. It actually got to the stage where he couldn't even eat a meal in peace and he had to resort to having his food in the seclusion of his cell. It had taken a couple of days for the reality to sink in that he would soon be free but in the meantime Davey knew there was a lot to do, both legally and illegally. Tony Smart, Davey's solicitor, was ordered to make a visit to The Scrubs where he was informed that he was to instruct a new Barrister, in fact Davey wanted a complete legal team hired to make sure there were no slip ups and the appeal would go ahead without a hitch. Tony Smart was also told to leak the story to the media so that there would be no delay as Davey knew another miscarriage of justice was the last thing the government needed at a time when there was already too much political unrest. He waited with baited breath for the morning tabloids to come out and as he hadn't yet subscribed to any newsagent, a must for anyone wanting to receive a daily paper while doing a stretch, he hoped there would be many willing to share their own. Davey needn't have worried as on his return from the shower block a copy of The Mail sat neatly folded on his bed. The headline filled the entire front page and Davey eagerly scanned the lines. There was no comment yet from the Met but Tony Smart had made sure that he was quoted word for word, which included a nice little piece just before the end, asking how many more innocent men would be sentenced by a corrupt judicial system?

Two days later the ball was well and truly in motion and swiftly after breakfast Davey Wiseman was escorted to one of the private interview rooms where he was greeted by his Solicitor, newly instructed Barrister and the man's Chamber Clerk.

"Good morning Mr Wiseman. My name is Hugo Urquhart and I will be representing you in The Court of Appeal. I have it on good authority that without question your conviction will be overturned.

Superintendent Loftwood was not alone when he recorded his involvement in your case. The video footage was actually taken at his home by none other than his wife so the evidence will not be questioned too deeply. I strongly advise you not to apply for bail at this moment in time as the case is moving so swiftly due to all the

media coverage that any application would indeed slow matters down."

"So how long am I looking at here, a few months, a year maybe?"

Hugo Urquhart QC smiled as he answered but Davey knew the man's friendliness was false and only in place because of the five figure retainer he was being paid.

"I'm pleased to say nowhere near as long as that. The government want this to go away as quickly as possible so I am assuming that it should all be done and dusted within two weeks."

Davey began to pace the room. He couldn't believe what was happening, a few days ago he was looking at spending years in this shit hole and now he could be back

12

home in Mayfair by the end of the month.

"As soon as we have a date Mr Smart will inform you but there really is very little for you to do but wait. Goodbye Mr Wiseman and I'm sure that the next time we meet you will be a free man."

The visitors were about to leave when Davey leant forward and grabbing Tony Smart's arm, whispered into the man's ear.

"Tell Barry McCann I want to see him pronto, see if you can wangle a visit for tomorrow."

The men then left and Davey was escorted back to his cell but nothing could wipe the smile from his lips. It was all about to kick off and he couldn't wait to get started. Shauna had only been a blip in his life and the upset she had caused could have been far worse, that said, he wasn't going to be lenient, she had fucked him over and it was now time to pay the piper. He thought about her cooped up in that solitary room and wondered just what was going through her mind. Lying on his bed he began to think of ways to make her suffer, in the beginning and on his first few nights in this hell hole, it had been a simple decision, she had to die but now things were once more in his favour, he wanted to have some fun before her finale.

Barry McCann didn't like being summoned by anyone but then again, Davey Wiseman wasn't just anyone. He hated The Scrubs and avoided being there at any cost, even when one of his own boys got banged up he refused to visit. Today was different, today one of the hardest gangsters in London wanted to see him and he wasn't about to refuse the request. The two men had occasionally done business in the past or at least that's how Barry liked to refer to it. In reality it was a case of carrying out some distasteful work on the big man's behalf. Barry wasn't exactly small time but for some reason he had never managed to reach the major league. It might have been the fact that he didn't want to move out of Edmonton but more likely that he held the social skills of a gnat when it came to dealing with people.

After booking in and then being escorted to the visiting room Barry waited anxiously for Davey to appear. He couldn't think of any reason as to why he'd been asked here as he'd carried out Davey's instructions to the letter and the woman was still being securely held. The door at the end of the room opened and as the prisoners filed in he knew he was about to find out if he was in deep shit or not. Davey ambled up to the table and after taking a seat eyed the man with a steely glare for a few seconds.
"Alright Mr Wiseman?"
Davey nodded his head but still didn't speak which as hard as he was, unnerved Barry. Finally when he couldn't stand the silence any longer and was just about to babble out some inane sentence Davey spoke.
"How is she?"
"Who?"
Davey's eyes narrowed, he wasn't sure if the man was thick or just trying to be funny but either way he wasn't in the mood to fuck around.
"Don't be a cunt McCann you know exactly who I mean."
"She's fine, you don't need to worry Mr Wiseman but things could get a bit difficult when she's ready to fucking drop I can tell you."
"What the fuck are you on about?"

Suddenly the penny dropped for Barry. Davey Wiseman, The Davey Wiseman, hadn't got a clue about the girl's condition.

"You didn't know she was up the duff Mr Wiseman? Well and truly up the fucking duff if you want my opinion."

For a moment Davey's bottom jaw felt like it was about to hit the floor. He could count on one hand the times he'd been speechless and this was definitely one of those times. Exhaling and puffing out his cheeks he slowly moved his head from side to side.

"How far gone?"

"Well I ain't no doctor but I'd say she's due any day now."

Davey quickly did the maths in his head and his face instantly turned ashen. Beckoning to one of the screws he asked for the use of a pen and something to write on. While the officer waited Davey quickly scribbled down a number and a list of items before passing the pen back and when the two men were alone again he handed the paper over to Barry McCann.

"Phone this number and ask for an appointment. The person's name is Stan."

"Stan who?"

"Are you trying to wind me up on fucking purpose you cunt?"

"No Mr Wiseman, sorry I can be a thick twat at times."

"You will be told where to meet them, now listen fucking carefully to what I want. Tell Stan I need a long range remote close surveillance camera set up, the kind that can be recorded. Promise Stan anything, no matter what the cost is. I'll be out of here in a couple of weeks so say I'll sort the cash out when I get back. So?"

"So what?"

"Get fucking out of her you daft cunt, oh and Barry?"

"Yes Mr Wiseman?"

"Don't fucking let me down. If everything goes well then I will owe you, if it doesn't then you will owe me and believe you me Barry, you really really, don't want to be in my debt."

Davey stood up from the table, turned and walked towards the rear of the room and as Barry McCann watched him leave he could feel the perspiration as it dripped from his brow. The stories of what vicious acts Davey Wiseman and Billy Jackson had carried out were legendary across London and well, Barry actually knew first hand, had personally witnessed what they were capable of and there was nothing fictitious in the rumours.

Now back in Edmonton and seated in The Ace, Barry McCann removed his mobile and nervously tapped in the number Davey had given to him. He didn't know what to expect and was a little taken aback when a woman answered the call.

"Could I speak to Stan sweetheart?"

"Stan speaking, how can I help?"

After the initial shock Barry explained that he was working on behalf of Davey Wiseman and then relayed the shopping list that Davey had requested. He was then informed that everything would be ready that evening, he was also told to be at the Texaco service station on Caledonian Road at 8pm sharp. Barry really didn't fancy the drive over to Islington, he hated North London and it would also mean that he wouldn't be able to have a beer. He was an early doors drinker and this was really going to mess up his schedule, still if it kept him in Davey's

16

good books it would be well worth it.

The forecourt was empty when he arrived but a few minutes later a shiny black Jaguar pulled up behind him. A woman stepped from the car and Barry's jaw dropped. She was tall, blonde and had legs right up to her armpits and he would bet money on it that her tits had been bought off the shelf. Opening the passenger side door she was soon sitting in the seat next to him and he gulped hard when she spoke in a thick Birmingham accent.

"What's your name love?"

"Barry, Barry McCann and I think I spoke to you earlier?"

The woman didn't offer her name and only nodded as she opened up a small briefcase that was perched on her lap. The case was purpose made and snapping open the lid she revealed a foam interior housing two micro cameras, a small electrical device that Barry didn't have the first idea what it was supposed to do and a row of memory sticks.

"Do you know how to operate a laptop?"

Barry was slightly offended with the fact that she was insinuating that he might look thick but then again, maybe she was right as he didn't have the first idea about technology and if asked he wouldn't even know how to turn a laptop on let alone operate one. The woman instantly read his thoughts and smiled.

"Not to worry love, I'll write it all down for you."

Scribbling away for a few moments she handed a sheet of paper along with the briefcase over to Barry and then casually stepped from the car without uttering another word.

The following day everything was put into place. Big

Igors installed the cameras into opposite corners of the farmhouse basement and a transit van had been parked up in the woods just over a mile away. The woman had informed Barry that any further distance and there would be a risk that the signal could break up. A large caravan battery was positioned inside the van to power a laptop. The computer would remain in sleep mode unless any movement occurred, if it did then images would be picked up and transmitted by the cameras back to the laptop. When Shauna was sleeping, which was most of the time, there would be little drain on the battery and it was now Ray's job to check the charge every day and if it was low then a replacement was to be put into place. A memory stick had been inserted to copy any captured images but he was under strict instructions not to view anything that had been recorded. After he had called in on Shauna, given her food for the day, checked the battery and changed the memory stick in the van, he was to report straight back to his boss.

Mindful of the warning she had received, Shauna had watched Igors put the cameras up in silence and the man had made sure they were positioned high enough so that she couldn't tamper with them. She stubbornly remained seated in the armchair after the two men had gone and looking around she then glanced in the direction of one of the cameras and stuck up two fingers. The only comfort she got was the hope that the devices might have been installed for when she eventually went into labour, or at least that was what she was praying for.

CHAPTER THREE

It had been almost two weeks since Shauna's abduction but since her girl walked out, to Jackie Silver it might as well have been a year. Her heart ached with longing for the young woman and until now she had never realised that emotional pain could be so intense and hurt so much, maybe even more than physical pain. Oh she was used to Shauna disappearing, she had left Jackie a couple of times over the years but this time it was different, this time she had thought they would be together forever. Jackie had made plans and they weren't short term ones, she had daydreamed about helping raise the baby and now she had nothing to look forward to. Checking the answer phone on both her landline and mobile, never mind emails and texts, anything in the slim hope that Shauna had left a message became a nigh on hourly ritual and it was starting to take over her life but in reality Jackie knew her girl wasn't coming back, wasn't going to walk through the front door and call out her usual 'I'm home!' The house was now always deathly quiet and Jackie would spend most of her time just sitting in her chair reminiscing as she shed many a tear. The only sound she would allow in the bungalow was having the radio on for the news and one morning in particular the words she heard would change her life forever. As usual, after making tea and toast for her breakfast she had taken her seat and turned on the Bush radio, it was a replica of an old one that she used to have back in the sixties. When the newsreader began to read out the headlines she instantly dropped the cup she was holding onto the floor. Its contents splashed everywhere but Jackie made no attempt to clean it up. Hardly daring to breathe she instantly froze and instead listened intently to what was being said.

"Late yesterday afternoon, notorious London gangster David Yosef Wiseman was released from prison. His appeal was successful after the revelation that irrefutable new evidence had come to light. Wiseman, serving fifteen years for his alleged part in the criminal activity of attempting to supply drugs on a national scale, had apparently been set up by a high ranking member of The Metropolitan Police Force. At 6pm on the steps of the Old Bailey Wiseman's solicitor Tony Smart read out a statement in which he called for further investigation into this gross miscarriage of justice.

A response from The Met is expected to be announced later today."

Jackie couldn't believe what she was hearing and suddenly her longing for Shauna turned to extreme fear. This evil man that had caused her girl so much pain was once again walking the streets and Shauna, wherever she was, would never be safe again. Jackie racked her brains as she tried to think of what to do but she didn't have a clue. The world these people lived in was so far removed from anything she knew and there was no one she could ask for help, or was there? Suddenly the image of sitting with her girl, on the night she saw the advertisement placed by that Gilly bloke when he was asking Shauna to get in touch filled Jackie's mind. Standing up too quickly she had to stop for a moment. Blood rushed to her head and for a second she felt dizzy but nothing would stop her trying to help. Jackie steadied herself by grabbing onto the fireplace and after taking several deep breaths she slowly walked over to the bureau. She didn't know why she had clipped the piece from the paper and tucked it away but there must have been a reason. It was a long shot, this Gilly person might have changed his number but with no other avenue open to her she picked up her phone, tapped in the number and waited with baited breath for him or someone else to answer. Gilly was now in Florida as he had reasoned that should they look, then it was a safe enough distance away that Davey's men would have difficulty in finding him. With the time distance five hours earlier than in the UK, he was still tucked up in bed when his mobile began to ring. Rubbing his eyes he grabbed the phone and peered at the screen, there was no name and not recognising the number he was reluctant to answer and switched the cut off button. When the line went dead Jackie redialled, she was angry that she'd been disconnected but at the same time she was optimistic as the line was still obviously in use which at least gave her some hope.

Swinging his legs over the side of the bed Gilly sat up and studied his mobile as it blared out the tune of 'You can ring my bell' by Donna Summer. No matter what mood he was in the song always made Gilly smile, well, that was until today. It was the same number calling and he suddenly had a sinking feeling in the pit of his stomach that something was very very wrong. Sighing deeply he knew that he had to answer.

"Hello?"

"Is that Gilly?"

"Depends who's asking?"

The relief Jackie felt couldn't be described and when she began to speak she had to brush away a tear as it fell onto her cheek.

"My Name is Jackie Silver, you don't know me but we have a mutual friend that I think might been in need of your help."

As soon as the woman stated her name Gilly knew exactly who the mutual friend was. When Shauna had revealed her life story to him there had been so much love whenever she had mentioned the woman, that her name had for some reason unknown to him, became well and truly lodged in his brain."

"I know who you are and its Shauna you're referring to isn't it?"

"Oh Mr Gilly she's in so much trouble and...."

For a second he smiled but it was only momentarily, just the mention of Shauna had his heart doing somersaults.

"It's not Mr Gilly, Gilly is my first name, well actually it's not it's, anyway that's beside the point. What's going on and how is she?"

Jackie didn't know the man but she did have a feeling that she could trust him. Shauna had talked about him with real feeling and Jackie thought that in another life, he would probably have been perfect for her girl but that was all hypothetical and the only thing on her mind was trying to make sure Shauna and her baby were safe.

"As of last night Davey Wiseman was a free man and..."

There was a strange noise on the other end of the line as Gilly dropped his phone in shock. Scrambling around on the bedside rug he quickly retrieved it and a second later she heard him speak but his breath was rapid.

"Free? Whatever are you talking about?"

"His conviction was overturned, seems he was set up. All a bit suspicious if you ask me but then what do I know about such things? Anyway, Shauna left for, well I don't know where exactly but she left all the same, about, well it must be almost two weeks ago now. I wouldn't be worried as she's done it before but well you know the score Gilly. Do you have any way of getting in touch with her?"

"Only an old mobile number but it was disconnected before she left London so that's a dead end."

The line was silent for several seconds as they were both absorbed in their own thoughts. Jackie was the first to speak and her next sentence shocked Gilly Slade to the core.

"Her baby is due any day and I just need to know she's safe and being looked after."

Jackie had chosen her words carefully as she knew there was a slim chance that Shauna was actually with the man and if that was the case she didn't want to risk being cut off again.

"Baby!!! You mean she's pregnant?"

There was no faking his shock and surprise and Jackie instantly knew that she was barking up the wrong tree with her previous idea.

"Yes Gilly she is. She must have been about three months gone when she arrived here, admittedly she didn't know but it soon became apparent when the morning sickness started. Neither of us were best pleased I can tell you but we soon came around to the idea, after all it's an innocent baby we're talking about, a baby that has had no part in all that happened. You've obviously guessed that Wiseman is the father?"

"Does he know? That was a stupid question, no of course he doesn't."

"So what do I do Gilly?"

Taking a moment he racked his brains trying to think of something but his thoughts hit a brick wall at every turn. He wouldn't turn his back, he couldn't, the love he felt for her still burned like a volcano.

"I don't know yet but you have my number and I now have yours. Give me a couple of days to think of something and then I'll get in touch. Thank you Jackie."
"What for?"
"For asking for my help and giving me the chance to maybe see her again. When I left England I knew it wasn't the end but I had hoped that should our paths ever cross again it would be on a happier note. Still there's no point in thinking about what might have been, I have work to do if I'm to try and save our girl."
With that the line went dead and Jackie couldn't help the smile that formed on her lips. She had liked the words 'our girl' and knew that this man would do whatever it took to bring Shauna home.

When Davey Wiseman walked into The Pelican Janice was in the middle of bottling up. The previous evening Tony Smart had called at her flat over in Somers Town and asked her to reopen the club as soon as possible. He hadn't given a reason only the fact that it was on Davey's instruction. Glancing up Janice did a double take, she was about to say that they weren't open but Davey's broad grin saw her run around from the bar and in seconds she was embracing her boss.
"Well you're a fucking sight for sore eyes and no mistake."
"Ain't you seen the news Jan?"
"No I ain't had the telly on I was too excited about getting back to this dive."
They both laughed but as quickly as it arrived the laughter disappeared when Davey's face turned solemn.
"You seen anything of that cunt Gilly Slade?"
Now Janice was fearful, she loved her boss but she was,

in a strange kind of way, also very fond of Gilly.
"Ain't seen hide nor hair of him, not since the day he closed up this place. What's the daft fucker done this time?"
One look from Davey and she knew that whatever it was it was serious, Janice also knew that she shouldn't ask any more question, she'd spent enough years in her boss's employment and on a day like today she didn't want to get in his bad books.
"I'll be in the office but unless it's a matter of life and death I don't want to be disturbed. Let me know when you want to get off home and I'll come and lock the front door."
Janice nodded her head and before she had chance to walk back around the bar her boss had disappeared into his office. Davey looked remarkably well considering and why he'd got a bee in his bonnet she didn't have the foggiest but as she bent down and began to replenish the bottles she couldn't get Gilly out of her head. Now Janice had a dilemma, be disloyal to Davey and possibly save the other man's life or stay loyal and remain silent. Deep down she knew the answer, she'd seen her boss's angry expression too many times over the years and when he was like this someone always suffered. Janice had an idea that Gilly Slade, for whatever he may or may not have done, might not survive this one and Davey could be planning his revenge right at this very moment. Making her way to the ladies toilet, the only area in this place where she was guaranteed some privacy, she removed a mobile from the pocket of her jeans and after a few seconds of hesitation she tapped in Gilly's number. This time when Donna Summer began to sing Gilly Slade grinned.

"Jan! How the fuck are you girl?"

"How the fuck am I? Gilly what the hell have you done, you do know Davey's out and on the fucking war path?"

Gilly had to play it cool and act as if he didn't have a clue what she was on about.

"Out! Are you pulling my plonker or something?"

"Of course I'm not but I suggest you lay low for a bit or are you coming back?"

"Jan, I'm lying around a pool in thirty three degrees as we speak, would you come back?"

Gilly was once again being economical with the truth and was still in bed but he reasoned that if she was about to stab him in the back and relay to Davey everything that had been said, then they would be looking at countries far away from where he actually was. Janice hadn't answered and he saw it as his opportunity to end the call.

"Well I have to get going as it's my turn to get the not so alcohol free Nom Yen in. Bye for now and tell the boss I won't be seeing him any time soon."

Gilly cut the line and ran his hand through his hair in frustration. He prayed that if she was going to tell tales then Davey would think he was in Thailand. Gilly had heard the name Nom Yen, a Thai drink made from syrup and hot milk on one of the holiday programmes and now hoped it would lead them on a wild goose chase but whatever happened he knew it wouldn't be long before he was on the move again and with Shauna now in grave danger, Gilly Slade had an idea that cold wet Blighty might soon be his next destination.

CHAPTER FOUR

On the fifteenth day of her imprisonment Shauna woke
with a start and shot bolt upright, which was difficult in
her condition. She didn't know the time or even what
day it was but as she slowly got up from the camp bed a
gush of water released itself like a torrent from between
her legs. Instantly she was in a blind panic, her waters
had broken, the baby was on its way and there was no
one there to help her. Slowly walking into the corner of
the room she stared up at one of the cameras and as she
began to cry she mouth the words 'Help me please!!!!'
over and over again but there was no response. A
niggling twinge started to hurt in her side and it soon
escalated to pain like she had never experienced before.
Shauna felt like she wanted to go to the toilet but at the
same time knew it was the baby coming and not the need
to release her bowels. She started to pace the floor trying
to ease the pain, God she didn't even have a watch or
clock to time her contractions. Bending over she
struggled to pick up the book that Ray had given to her
and began to flick through its pages. When she read that
a first labour could last for hours the tears came thick and
fast. Somehow pacing the floor she tried to count but
with every stabbing pain she lost what number she had
gotten too. Now with her hands clasped onto the back of
the old armchair she panted, her breathing became harder
every time a fresh onslaught of contractions began and
her nails dug so hard into the fabric that she left nail
marks. Shauna was in the middle of a new wave of pain
when she heard the basement door open. Ray Harvey
was by her side in seconds and the look of concern on his
face told Shauna that he wasn't all bad, that he could at

least feel other people's pain and emotion.

"Come on let's get you moving, when my wife was at this stage she found it best to walk about, kind of like walking through the pain if you know what I mean?"

Shauna took his hand and as he placed his arm around her they slowly stepped around the room. Ten minutes later and the contractions suddenly stopped.

"There! Panic over, it was probably Branson Haps."

From out of nowhere Shauna began to laugh and Ray gave her a quizzical look.

"I think you mean Braxton Hicks and it's definitely not those as my waters have broken."

"Oh, right then, so what do we do now?"

Again Shauna wanted to laugh but at the same time she was grateful that she had someone with her even if he didn't have a clue about what to do.

"Not a lot I can do is there? This baby will come when it's ready and not before. I suppose I should make the most of it and rest up but I'm so scared. You won't leave me will you?"

Ray puffed out his cheeks. He hadn't signed up for this and if Barry found out what he was doing, well he'd hit the roof. Ray took a moment to mull over the options and then coming to a decision he turned to face the now desperate young woman.

"Look darlin', I can't stay here. My cunt of a boss will have my guts for garters if he finds out I'm even talking to you."

Shauna was about to protest, about to plead if that was what it would take but she was stopped when he suddenly grabbed her hand and stared deep into her eyes.

"I ain't finished yet. Now you obviously know what those cameras are for."

It was a rhetorical question and Ray didn't give Shauna time to answer.

"Every movement you make is recorded and I have to collect those recordings every day. If I get caught helping you, well I don't even want to think about that darlin' but I ain't as evil as you might think I am and there's no way I'm willing to leave you high and dry. I'm going to watch today's recording live and if I think you really can't cope then I'll be back here in a matter of minutes. I know it ain't what you want but believe you me sweetheart, it's the best offer you're gonna get and I really am taking a risk here."

Fleetingly images of Davey and Billy filled her mind and Shauna knew exactly what the man meant and what could happen to him if anyone ever found out he had helped her. Straining to get to her feet she kissed him on the cheek and said 'Thank you'. Tough guy Ray Harvey suddenly got embarrassed and taking a step backwards coughed loudly.

"Right, that's enough of all that malarkey. I need to get off now but remember, it's going to hurt like hell and it'll feel as if your guts are being ripped out but that's the way of the world and a woman's cross to bear I'm afraid."

Turning, Ray headed towards the stairs but as he placed his foot on the first tread he called over his shoulder.

"Don't forget I'll be keeping an eye on you."

Shauna collapsed back down in the armchair with a thud and sighed heavily, so this was it, this was how the most precious memory she was ever going to have would be remembered. Still, she supposed it could have been worse, she could have been giving birth out in the wilds like some poor Ethiopian woman and suddenly she laughed at her own sorry position, would that have been any worse than this?

The hours ticked by and she didn't know if it was night or day. She wasn't hungry and apart from having to pee every half an hour everything seemed to have gone quiet. The thought had only just entered her head when the most excruciating pain raged through her body and as quickly as she could Shauna stood up, walked behind the chair and gripped the headrest as tightly as she could. Opening her legs was a natural instinct and with one hand she struggled to remove her knickers. Bending her legs slightly Shauna suddenly felt compelled to push and with gritted teeth she bore down as hard as she could. A few seconds later and the pain subsided but she knew this was only the beginning. Panting heavily she began to count again but at the two minutes mark the pain once more ripped through her. The book had been informative and she was now more grateful to the man for giving it to her than he would ever know. Shauna couldn't control the urge to push and her vagina felt as if it was being split in two. Staring up at the ceiling she willed Vonny to help her, pleaded with her sister not to desert her now, not in her moment of need but there was nothing, absolutely nothing at all. As she panted and pushed she could suddenly feel the head emerge from between her legs and she screamed out in agony. Staggering over to the camp bed she somehow managed to lay down onto her back. Contraction after contraction ripped through her body and Shauna was bathed in sticky sweat but she didn't care, all that she could think about was delivering her child safely. Just when she though she couldn't take anymore the next onslaught began and with one final push the shoulders emerged. In the next few seconds her baby was born and

Shauna sobbed with happiness and relief. Reaching down into the box of tricks that Ray had brought her she desperately tried to remember all that she had read in the book. Shauna quickly opened the sterile clamps and scissors and attaching two of the plastic clamps to the umbilical cord she used the small scissors to separate her baby from its life force. Suddenly she realised that she didn't even know what sex her child was and stopping for a moment she peered down to discover that she was now the mother of the most beautiful baby girl. Shauna carefully lifted her tiny child up and after wrapping her in a towel, held her close while at the same time rubbing up and down the spine until her baby began to cry.

"You really are the most beautiful precious thing I have ever seen. Welcome to the world little Jacqueline, you know something? I think I'm going to call you JJ for short. Your aunty Jacks would have loved that. You won't get to know her I'm afraid, not her or your daddy but he was a bad man JJ, still, I loved him even after everything he did and is still doing to me."

Laying JJ down at the foot of the bed Shauna knew that she had to now deliver the placenta. The book had stated that it could be a tricky procedure and if something went wrong or it wouldn't come out then she hadn't got a clue what would happen. Glancing in the direction of the camera she gave a weak smile in the hope that Ray was being true to his word and watching her closely. Again the contractions began but this time it was quick and simple and the sac of nourishment that had sustained her baby for the last nine months swiftly left her body. JJ was now crying as loudly as her little lungs would allow and Shauna knew that she was hungry. Sitting up at the best angle she could manage she opened up her blouse

31

and laid the baby onto her breast. Aware of the camera, Shauna turned her body as much as she was able. Her modesty had now returned and she hated the thought that some man was watching her. Seated in the Transit van and over a mile away Ray Harvey couldn't take his eyes off of the screen. He had never been witness to anything so brave or beautiful in his life before. True he'd been in attendance when all of his kids had come into the world and the last one had been tricky to say the least but it was still within the safety of a hospital. This, well this was fantastic! Shauna must have been so scared and yet she had delivered her baby alone and without complication. Ray knew that for the rest of his life he would never be witness to anything as wonderful as this again. Dawn had broken over an hour earlier and after removing the memory stick he left the van but didn't head straight back to London. Instead he returned to the farmhouse and as he descended the staircase Shauna's smile lit up the basement.

"Well done darlin' I knew you could do it."

"Isn't she beautiful?"

Ray peered into the baby's face and he had to admit that with her mop of jet black hair and rosebud lips she really was a stunner.

"Yes she is sweetheart, takes after her mum I expect."

"A bit I suppose but I can see Davey in her."

Ray took a step back and Shauna could see that he was shocked.

"It okay, I'm not about to deny that he's the father and anyway, she's the one good thing to come out of our relationship though what he'll say when he finds out I really don't know. I'm not so frightened for myself but I just pray to God that he won't let any harm come to her."

32

"Darlin', there really ain't no worries on that score. I ain't met a man yet who when seeing his own child, his flesh and blood, especially when they're new born, would hurt a hair on their heads."

"That's what I'm trying to say, she won't be a new born when he sees her will she? She'll be getting ready to leave school by the time he's released."

Ray Harvey licked his lips, swallowed hard and stared at the ground wishing it would swallow him up. Shauna instantly knew he was holding something back and she could feel the onset of panic.

"What, what is it? Ray!!"

"Look I don't even know if it's the truth but there's a rumour going round London, well the part of London that I frequent anyway. They reckon he's out, got off on some technicality or something. My boss ain't said anything and in the line of work I'm in, well you don't ask too many questions sweetheart, not if you want to keep a tongue in your head."

Shauna ran her hand through her hair as she tried to think of something she could do but she was a prisoner and was incarcerated here at Davey's will.

"He won't take her away from me will he? I couldn't bare it if he took her, oh please tell me he won't!"

As hard as he was, Ray, felt as if his heart was breaking. This poor woman was not only being held against her will, for Christ sake she'd just given birth and now she was scared shitless that some gangster was about to take her baby. The only problem was the fact that Ray couldn't reassure her, couldn't tell her that everything would be alright because he knew the chances were that they wouldn't be. Davey Wiseman was a nasty bastard and if he thought he could cause her pain then he would and that was without the fact that the kid was his. Shauna's eyes were still pleading for reassurance and he knew that as much as it went against the gain, a lie was called for.

"Darlin' of course he won't. He wouldn't have the first clue of how to look after a baby and I'd say this has put you in a much better position. I reckon when he sees her he will have a complete change of heart."

"You think so, you really think that might happen?"

"Sure I do, now I have to get off back to the smoke so you rest up and take care of that little one."

Ray left the house with a heavy heart, men like Wiseman had no feeling or conscience and there was a distinct possibility that the young woman could be dead and buried within a week. Back in the basement Shauna was thinking the exact same thing, she knew how Davey worked and for what she had done to him he would want to hurt her as much as was humanly possible.

CHAPTER FIVE

Some forty eight hours had passed since Davey's release but the journalists were still camped outside his home. He had been advised by his solicitor not to give a statement and as he stared out over Hyde Park he once again felt like a prisoner. The surroundings of his apartment were luxurious beyond words but it was a prison all the same and it was the first time he'd spent any length of time at home without Fran being there. At the thought of her he laughed to himself, he didn't think he would ever get to grips with referring to her as Shauna. Memories flooded back of their time together and a dull ache filled his heart. Raising his arms above his head Davey stretched out and suddenly felt the rage as it began to take over his mind. All the hurt she had caused, was still causing in fact, well it couldn't be left unpunished. He was still in love with her, craved her touch and her tenderness but all the same she had to pay!

It was lunchtime when Barry McCann made his way to The Ace. The place was busy but as usual no one dared to sit in his seat. Walking over to the bar he ordered a scotch and within seconds was deep in thought. With all the media coverage he was now overly nervous about being connected to Davey Wiseman but there was no way he could drop the job he was doing for the man, well not unless he wanted to be branded gutless and that would definitely have finished his criminal career, not to mention the fact that he would be forced to experience Davey's wrath. Glancing at his watch he realised that Ray was late which was unusual and in Barry's book not a good sign.

After leaving Shauna, Ray Harvey, instead of going to see his boss, had returned home. Something about what he had witnessed this morning made him want to see his own family and as he walked through the front door he was greeted with screaming and the sound of loud music. The noise didn't bother him in the least, it was normal for this household and it actually made him feel better. Entering the kitchen he saw his wife standing at the sink washing up, there was no such luxury as a dishwasher in their household as it took every penny just to feed them all. Little Danny, the youngest of the Harvey clan, was pulling on his mother's leggings. Snot was streaming from his nose in two thick candles and all he wanted was a cuddle from a woman who never seemed to get a minute to herself. Ray scooped the boy up into his arms, wiped the child's nose with his sleeve and then lent in to give his wife a kiss.

"You're back early?"

"Just a flying visit babe, I'm meant to be at The Ace as we speak but I just wanted to see you for a minute."

Sally eyed her husband with suspicion. Ray was a good man and a fine provider but he was also a bit of a dreamer and that's what had seen him banged up for a two stretch. He'd only been home a few months and Sally was constantly worrying that he was up to no good again.

"What are you hanging around that fucking dive for?"

"Because my Angel, that's where I have to meet Barry and if I don't show then I won't get paid and ergo we won't be able to feed the kids. Where are they by the way?"

"Ray junior's round at your mums, Abi's gone shopping and Britney's up in her room in a fucking strop but then

what's new? I'm surprised you didn't hear that bleeding racket she's playing? You want a cuppa?"
"Oh go on then but it'd better be a quick one."
The couple chatted away with ease, it was one of the reasons they had stayed so close throughout all the crap that had been thrown at them over the years, everything between them was always so comfortable and easy. As Ray glanced up at the clock and saw that it was now ten thirty he shot up from the chair.
"Fuck my old boots! Look at the time!"
"Another cuppa?
"Nah best not, if I don't get over to Barry soon Britney won't be the only one in a strop."

Ray Harvey arrived at The Ace forty minutes later and he knew by the look on his boss's face that his premonition had come to fruition.
"And what fucking time do you call this?"
Ray knew it was a statement more than a question and he mouthed the word 'sorry'. Handing over a bag containing the memory sticks that had been recorded over the last week he hung around waiting to be paid.
"What?"
"My wages?"
Barry McCann threw a wad of twenty pound notes down onto the bar and with a look of distaste walked from The Ace and hailed a cab. He'd agreed to meet Davey in The Pelican at eleven and he was already half an hour late. Walking towards the club Barry was oblivious to the two reporters who were leant up against a car bonnet and pushing open the front door, he walked over to the bar and asked Janice if her boss was in. Within minutes he was shown to Davey's inner sanctum and was soon

standing in front of the big man's desk feeling like a naughty school boy. Davey removed the sticks, held them in his hand and after studying Barry for a few seconds, which made the man feel increasing nervous, he handed over a manila envelope.

"Nice work, now keep them coming."

"Are you sure about all of this Mr Wiseman? I mean if anyone gets a sniff of what's going on you could end up back inside, well come to that we all could."

"You got the wind up McCann, losing your bottle?"

Barry resented the insinuation but knew better than to argue, Davey was a player and as much as Barry wanted to be in the big league this man scared him shitless. Turning to leave the office he was momentarily stopped by Davey's final sentence.

"Don't ever fucking think about shafting me McCann."

Barry vigorously shook his head and then left The Pelican as quickly as his legs would carry him. His tardiness had put Wiseman in a bad mood and it was all because of that cunt Ray Harvey, well Barry would be having words with that little bastard and they wouldn't be pleasant, that was for sure.

Davey dropped the memory sticks into his jacket pocket. The club wasn't a safe place to view them and he couldn't wait much longer to see her face again. Janice was still behind the bar polishing bottles and glancing in her boss's direction she waited for a goodbye but there was nothing. Whatever was going on Davey didn't look happy and that didn't bode well for anyone. Momentarily she thought of Gilly and hoped that whatever was going down didn't include him. After Davey and Billy had been sentenced she'd thought it was the end of the line for herself and all the other employees so when Tony Smart had rocked up at her home and reinstated her, Janice had been over the moon. Now she had a sinking feeling in the pit of her stomach as she realised that getting her job back might turn out to only be short term. Exiting through the rear door Davey was soon back in his apartment. Entering through the underground garage he'd been able to avoid the press but he knew that sooner or later he would get cornered and he now wished that Tony Smart hadn't read out the statement but at the time he'd been angry and was only now able to think straight. Then again, any high profile case that got overturned by the Court of Appeal would still have hit the headlines so he supposed all this media attention was inevitable after all. For no reason he closed the blinds in his study, poured a large a scotch and look a seat in the massive leather office chair. Davey was nervous, nervous at seeing the only woman who had ever managed to get inside his head and he didn't like the feeling. Switching on his laptop he noticed his hand was shaking as he pushed in the small piece of metal that would momentarily reunite him with Shauna. Stan had done well and the image and sound quality were spot on, it was almost as if he was watching a movie. When he saw the surroundings she was being kept in, he frowned and slowly shook his head but it was nothing compared to what he felt when he saw her face. Fran, his Fran, was dirty and unkempt. The raven hair that had replaced her copper locks hung greasy and limp around her shoulders but to him she was still stunning. He flicked through the first few days of recordings and when he saw the interaction between her and someone he would later find out to be Ray Harvey, Davey started to get angry.

That wanker McCann, had been given strict instructions that there should be no conversations to take place. He had wanted her in solitary confinement so she could think long and hard about what she'd done but McCann, like most of the tossers' he had to deal with, had employed someone else to do his dirty work. He was now vulnerable again as the more people who knew what was going on, the more chance there was of someone blabbing. Removing his mobile he quickly found the number and tapped his fingers in frustration while he waited for Barry to answer. Back in The Ace, Barry McCann had called Ray and summoned the man to another meeting so when his phone began to ring he didn't look at the screen and automatically assumed it was his employee.

"Don't fuck me about Ray, just get your arse down here pronto."

"What the fuck are you on about?"

"Oh sorry Mr Wiseman I thought you was someone else."

"I need to see you."

"You want me to come back to your club?"

"No, I'll come to you. Still frequenting that shit hole over in Edmonton?"

"Yes Mr Wiseman."

"Wait there for me then."

With that the line went dead and Barry McCann felt the first stirrings of fear. These men hardly ever ventured out of their own manor unless forced, so whatever Wiseman wanted it must be serious. Barry wasn't bright enough to realise that it was a simple case of avoiding the press but then that was the reason there were big boys like Wiseman and small fish like McCann.

Davey poured himself another drink before resuming the footage but whenever Shauna had to use the makeshift toilet he found himself looking away from the screen. She couldn't see him, didn't even know he was watching this but still, deep down he respected her and even if it was only in his own mind he had to give her privacy. Watching the saga of the rat unfold and the skills she had used to save her food made him smile, she was bright alright, too bright in fact and if she'd only planned things a little better at the end, Davey knew she would still be a free woman.

Pushing the last stick into the machine he sat back to watch. There was that strange man again only this time he was carrying a box. When Shauna kissed him on the cheek Davey's hands gripped the edge of the desk in frustration, fuck there would have to be a miracle for Barry to talk himself out of this one. Suddenly Davey bolted upright. The screaming was horrendous and he realised that right in front of his very eyes he was seeing the birth of his own child. With every contraction she had he could feel his own stomach tighten and when the baby was finally born he wiped away a tear from the corner of his eye and exhaled deeply.

Ray Harvey pushed open the main door to The Ace of Spades and slowly walked over to his boss. He wasn't exactly sure what he'd done wrong but the man's tone on the telephone had told him it was serious.

"What's up Boss?"

"Don't fucking what's up me! I told you to get here so I could give you a fucking slap for making me late and putting me in Wiseman's bad books but it now seems we've got a bigger problem on our hands."

"What's that then?"

"I don't know yet but he's coming over here."

"Who is?"

Barry shook his head, why oh why, did he surround himself with fucking Muppets all the time?

"Wiseman is, you daft cunt! Now before he gets here you better tell me what the fuck's been going on. Don't bother trying to be economical with the truth because the guy has the recording so if you've been doing anything you shouldn't have......"

Ray screwed up his face and it was a look that told Barry and anyone else in the vicinity that they may have a slight problem.

"What? What the fuck did you do Ray?"

"I didn't do anything, well not really. Look, the poor little cow was about to have her baby, what the fuck did..."

"Watch your mouth!"

"Sorry Mr McCann. What did you expect me to do? I just gave her a couple of bits to help her when the time came that's all."

Barry had his elbow on the bar and was now holding his head in his hand. This wasn't good, wasn't good at all and he didn't have the foggiest idea how the hell he was going to explain himself after he'd been given such strict instructions.   There was no time for any further dialogue between the two men as seconds later Davey Wiseman walked in. Taking a seat at the far end of the bar he beckoned for Ray to join him and Barry was relieved that he wasn't the one about to get aggravation. Ray slowly walked towards the man, a man that he'd never had any direct dealings with but who nonetheless instilled fear purely on the strength of his own name.

"Hello Mr Wiseman, how can I help you?"

"Take a pew."

Ray did as he was asked and the whole time his eyes never left those of the visitor.

"Right, I don't want any fucking spiel from you. I'm gonna ask questions and I want straight answers understood?"

"I ain't done nothing wrong I......."

"I said under- fucking - stood!"

"Yes Mr Wiseman understood."

"Now I know you've been checking in on the woman, how is she?"

Ray began to relay all that had happened. He explained about big Igors putting the cameras in place and how Shauna had pleaded with him for help. He said that she was doing good and that the baby was healthy and a real little stunner. Happy with the answers Davey dismissed the man and then made his way into the gent's toilets.

Ray almost ran over to where Barry was perched on a barstool, his face was as white as a sheet and he was sweating profusely.

"So? What did he want?"

There was no time for a reply and when they saw Davey walking over Barry swallowed hard.

"I hope everything's sorted now Mr Wiseman."

Swiftly and with no fuss Davey pulled out a small Glock handgun which he'd had tucked into the waist band of his trousers and rammed in into Barry's crotch.

"I warned you about trying to fuck me over McCann!"

As quick as a flash Davey released the safety catch and pulled the trigger. The chamber was empty but unaware of his Barry's bladder released itself.

"When I tell you to fucking do something you do it to the

43

fucking letter, understood?"

Barry could only nod his head vigorously and at the same time Ray took a step backwards but Davey quickly turned.

"Where are you off to cunt, I didn't tell you to fucking move did I?"

Both men were now paralysed with fear and Barry's eyes rapidly darted from Davey's face down to his own crotch, which was now soaked and then back up to Davey again. Removing the pistol, Davey grimaced with distaste when he noticed that the barrel was wet.

"You lily-livered cunt! Make sure you do as I say from now on or next time it will be loaded and I don't want him going anywhere near her again."

Ray's eyes opened wide but he remained as still as a statue. Davey walked from The Ace of Spades with a slight grin on his lips, these amateurs really were a fucking joke.

CHAPTER SIX

Within minutes of the news breaking that Davey Wiseman had been released, the outcome of the case had filtered down from the Crown Prosecution Service to Graham Myers. The Chief Inspector had been stunned and more than a tad pissed off when informed. For a second he could only think of his career and his own self-preservation. That thought was only fleeting and with the realisation of exactly what this could all mean, Graham wanted to be the one to personally reveal the news to his old friend. It wasn't a satisfactory outcome for the government, The Met but least of all for Neil Maddock. The man had worked tirelessly on the case and now he would be hung out to dry. It was common practise and one Graham had never cared to dwell on but this time it was different, this time it was personal and included his very dear friend. At Agar Street police station there was already another high profile investigation underway. Detectives and uniformed men moved swiftly through the corridors and boxes of papers and evidence were stacked high. Neil Maddock was the senior officer in charge and was in the middle of a morning update with his team when he was informed that there was an urgent telephone call.

"Not now Rod, can't you see I'm busy. Whoever it is, tell them to ring back later."

Neil's second in command Rodney Sheehan, quickly informed his guvnor that the person on the other end was a high ranking officer. Neil was still reluctant to take the call but knew better than to ignore one of the top brasses. Something as simple as a rebuff could see an invisible black mark go onto your record and the prospect of advancement in The Met would fly out of the window. Neil had already seen it happen to many fine detectives over the years, it wasn't fair but then life wasn't fair and you just had to suck it up.

"Maddock here?"

"Hi Neil, it's Graham."

"Hello Graham, ain't heard from you in a while my friend, what can I do for you?"

"I need you to come over to Scotland Yard as soon as possible."

"I'm a bit tied up at the moment, this afternoon any good to you?"

"Afraid not Neil, whatever you're doing will have to wait."

"Fair enough, I'm on my way!"

Detective Maddock couldn't see what the urgency was, maybe it was regarding his long overdue promotion or another high profile case but whatever it was he would find out soon enough. Things didn't go exactly to plan and when Neil returned to the incident room the team were all deathly silent, an odd occurrence in a normally buzzing office when the men were engrossed in a case and in a highly charged state. A large television which hung on the incident room wall and was used for all manner of screenings not to mention the latest news bulletin, had been strangely muted. By the look on his officers' faces, Neil knew something serious must have happened.

"What? Come on you lot, what's going on?"

Rodney Sheehan stepped forward and he wasn't looking forward to being the bearer of bad news but all of his colleagues had taken a step back when approached. One hearing the Court of Appeals decision, Detective

Inspector Neil Maddock was absolutely livid.

"You're having a fucking laugh ain't you? Oh no come on, please tell me it ain't true?"

Neil had waited years to catch Davey Wiseman and now the slippery bastard was once again walking the streets. Grabbing his coat and car keys he didn't utter another word to his team. Storming out of the station and driving at speed over to Westminster, he brought the car to a screeching halt in the car park of New Scotland Yard. Neil slammed the door hard and then ran up the steps to the entrance where the electronic doors seemed to mock him as they effortlessly glided open. Frustrated did not begin to describe how he was feeling, his patience was at breaking point and the rigorous security checks he was then forced to endure before he was allowed to enter, did little to calm the situation. As the meeting with Chief Inspector Myers had already been arranged, Neil took the lift up to the fourth floor and then barged straight into the office of his superior, his face red with rage.

"Have you heard? I don't fucking believe it! How the fuck did this happen Graham?"

For a moment the Chief Inspector was startled, this wasn't the kind of bad etiquette used at the Yard.

"Alright Detective calm down, I know it's not ideal but..."

Neil marched across the room and slammed the palm of his hand down onto the top of Graham's highly polished desk.

"Ideal! That wanker makes a mockery of the judicial system and you say it's not ideal?"

Chief Inspector Myers allowed his old friend some slack, no one ever barged into his office and dared to speak to him like this but today he was feeling generous.

Suddenly Neil remembered his rank and no matter how long the two had been friends, knew he had well and truly stepped over the invisible line of rank.

"I'm sorry Sir, I'm bang out of order and that wasn't called for."

"It's okay. Now for God's sake man, take a seat and calm down before you give yourself a bloody heart attack." Doing as he was asked Detective Maddock took a seat opposite the desk and could only shake his head in disbelief at the situation.

"You've heard the saying 'slowly slowly catchy monkey' Neil? Well Wiseman has slipped up before and he'll do it again. His sort always do, it's a foregone conclusion as they can't help themselves and besides, he hasn't got a guardian angel looking out for him this time."

"I realise that but fuck me Sir, it took me years to get him. It feels like he's laughing at us and that really sticks in my craw!"

"I'm well aware of that and it isn't going to look too good on my record either. I mean, I was the one that organised the arrest remember. When this farce starts to be investigated and believe you me it will, the Criminal Case Review Commission will leave no stone unturned. With Loftwood's damning admission, the only conclusion they can reach is inevitable and it won't be in our favour I can tell you. That means the ISOs will be coming after you, me as well come to that, so I really think you, we, have a lot more to worry about than Davey Wiseman being at liberty don't you?"

Neil sighed, shrugged his shoulders and reluctantly nodded his head. There was nothing he could do except wait and his boss was right, sooner or later Wiseman would put a foot wrong and Neil would be there ready and waiting to nab him. Well he would be if he still had a career in the force at the end of all of this.

By the time JJ was a week old Davey was viewing the recordings daily and it took all of his resolve not to go over to the farmhouse. He'd never had a maternal bone in his body until now but then this baby, this precious little being was a part of him, had his blood, his jet black hair and he was desperate to hold her but as deep as his feelings went for both mother and daughter, there was something holding him back. He couldn't forget what she had done to him and who she really was but then again, maybe it was a case of deep down he couldn't forget what he had done to her all those years ago. Until she'd revealed her true identity he hadn't really given Violet or her kids much thought but now they were constantly on his mind no matter how hard he tried to ignore the memories. While in prison the woman and her children had invaded his dreams nightly and since his release it was no different but Davey was strong in both mind and body and he wasn't about to allow his demons to beat him. Wanting and needing to stay under the radar of the police as he knew Maddock would be spitting feathers over the court's ruling, Davey had made the decision that as soon as he'd viewed the footage he would wipe the recordings. If there were no memory sticks then there would be no evidence against him regarding Shauna's kidnap should it ever come to light. The only stick he'd kept was the one of the baby's birth, it was special and he knew it was something he would never get to see again. Locked away in a safety deposit box at his bank, no one except him would ever know of its existence. After his warning to Barry McCann, Davey

49

had given further instructions that within reason, whatever Shauna asked for she could have. He wasn't going soft but at the same time he wanted his child cared for in the best way possible. Obviously the surroundings weren't ideal but they would have to do for now, at least until he could come up with alternative arrangements. Allowing her a few luxuries wouldn't do any harm and Davey had a feeling that all Shauna would ask for would be the essentials. After he'd been arrested it had crossed his mind that he didn't really know her at all but those thoughts had soon disappeared and she wasn't greedy, wasn't a woman out for material things, just someone who wanted revenge and all in all, not that different from himself really, a fact that had worried him a lot lately not that he would ever share that thought with anyone.

Shauna had taken to motherhood like a duck to water and the basement was now furnished with all the baby items she would ever need, well at least for the first few months but she prayed with all of her heart that they wouldn't be here that long. On his boss's instructions Big Igors asked if there was anything she wanted and Shauna had given him a list as long as her arm. When the stuff had started to arrive she knew Davey was behind it and wondered if he was watching her on the cameras. If he was then she hoped that he was aching for his child. It would at least be a way of getting out of her prison but then again she knew him too well, knew what he was capable of and he'd never had any love for children in the past so why should that change now? The only reason that she could possibly think of that could make a different from all those years ago, was the fact that JJ was his own flesh and blood. The thoughts racing through her mind now brought Vonny to the fore and Shauna hoped that her sister was at least watching over them from heaven. Along with a chemical toilet, water was now also in a plentiful supply which at least enabled her to wash and keep the baby clean. JJ was an angelic child who hardly cried and Shauna would spend hours just gazing into the baby's face. It saddened her that Ray was no longer sent to check on the two of them. She would never be privy to the fact that in the first few days he had called at the cottage daily when no one else was around. With his ear pressed tightly to the basement door, he had listened for any noise that would tell him mother and baby were fine. After his warning it would have been more than his life was worth to venture down the stairs or speak to her through the door as he'd either have been caught on camera or his voice would have been recorded and Davey would have been alerted. There was something about Ray, he reminded Shauna so much of Gilly Slade and she dearly wished that her friend was here now. Gilly would have saved them, got them out somehow and this could have all been so very different if she had only gotten to the airport like he had asked her to do. Still there was no point in crying over spilt milk, she just had to make the best of things, at least for now.

Igors Petrov stood just over six feet tall and was built like the proverbial brick shit house or that's how Barry McCann always referred to him. Considering he'd only arrived from Lithuania three years earlier, the man, much to his boss's relief had excelled in learning the English language. Igors was of Russian decent and when asked would state in a deep voice that he was Russian not Lithuanian, he might have been raised there but he hated all Lithuanians and saw them as an inferior people. Doing whatever was asked of him, which sometimes entailed unsavoury work, Igors was soon accepted into the small McCann firm but as macho as he appeared, there was a dark secret that Igors kept to himself, he loved men and the more effeminate they were the better. He was never seen with a woman and if the truth was told, he didn't like them, it was likely the reason that he had no problem when it came down to hurting them physically. Every day Igors would bring food to Shauna but he never spoke to her or paid any attention to the baby. When Shauna one day innocently moved towards the foot of the stair the man grabbed her roughly by the hair and pulled her backwards. Shauna was so frightened by his action that after that she would wrap JJ in her arms and sit silently in the armchair until he had gone. Out of the blue and only a couple of days later he suddenly stopped coming to the farmhouse and was replaced again by Ray, apparently Igors hadn't banked on Davey Wiseman seeing the assault but Davey would deal with him at a later date, for now he had more important matters to attend to.

CHAPTER SEVEN

While Davey basked in daily sunshine it was a completely different story on ward 12c at Broadmoor security hospital. After his conviction it hadn't taken long for Billy Jackson to be moved there. Specialists were called in and after several physiological tests had been carried out, he was diagnosed as criminally insane. It was never admitted by the powers that be but the diagnosis was in part down to the fact that no prison could control him. He was violent, sneaky and would do anything to disrupt the system. Now his daily routine was one of trying to hold on to the small amount of sanity he actually had left. Due to his psychotic behaviour and family history coming to light, Billy was being treated for schizophrenia but the real root cause of his behaviour was due to the contraction of HIV years earlier. Billy had not shared the information regarding his infection with another human being, not even Davey. His Harley Street doctor had been privately supplying a cocktail of drugs for years but the specialists at Broadmoor were not aware of the illness due to the fact that there were no NHS medical records. To anyone else Billy Jackson was the epitome of physical health. In the ensuing months and due to his lack of medication his illness would progress to full blown AIDS and the advancement of HIV associated dementia, known to the layman as AIDS mania. It would soon turn him into a jibbering wreck and there was no help available. For now and to all concerned he was just mad and he had a feeling he was going to enjoy his mental decline in the most spectacular way.

On his arrival at Broadmoor the ward nurse, a man

named Ashley Little, had taken an instant dislike to Billy.
On the outside Billy had been in charge but in here
Ashley was King of the Hill and ruled the ward with a
rod of iron, taking great pleasure in making the patients
suffer. Billy's legal team paid him a fortnightly visit, not
because they could actually help him in any way but
purely down to the fact that he held them on a large
monthly retainer. Lying on his bed one day, listening to
music on his iPod while desperately trying to blot out the
continual noise of people screaming and kicking off, he
was told that his visitors were here. Lionel Graves was a
solicitor and Mike Chapman his clerk. The men had been
sent from Bullman Associates and had been given the
unsavoury job of carrying out this particular task. The
staff from Bullmans', were under strict instructions to
always visit in pairs and to never make any kind of
statement that they were in a position to help the man.
Old Harry Bullman would have been more than happy to
forgo the money if it meant wiping Billy Jackson off of
his list of clients. There was just one problem, Harry
represented most of the criminal fraternity in the East
End of London and it was very lucrative for his company.
To drop Billy now would mean most of his clients
walking and it was something Harry wasn't prepared to
let happen. Today wasn't the norm and although still not
able to help Billy in any way, the solicitor had to inform
the man about Davey Wiseman's release.
"Jackson you've got visitors."
Billy didn't move and being ignored really riled nurse
Little. Storming over to the bed he kick it with force and
Billy bolted upright.
"What the fuck did you do that for you cunt?"
"I said you've got visitors now move your queer arse

before I move it for you."

Doing as he was told Billy headed towards the corridor that led to the main nurses' station but as he passed Ashley Little, he lent in as closely as he dared without being dropped to his knees.

"I won't always be in here, remember that you cunt because when I do eventually get out of this shit hole you'll be the first person on my list to visit."

"Yeah yeah, heard it all before Jackson, heard it all before. Now move your fucking arse or by God I'll make you pay when you get back on this ward."

Reluctantly Billy did as he was told, the nurse could wait until later, for now he was excited at the thought of having visitors even if they were only his legal representation. Entering a small room that was normally set aside for individual one on one therapy treatments, Billy as usual was full of bravado and proceeded to slap Lionel Graves hard on the back.

"How's it hanging mate?"

Although Lionel had been forewarned regarding the man's behaviour he was still taken aback and Mike Chapman, far senior in years to the solicitor, took a step towards the panic button which didn't go unnoticed by Billy.

"What the fuck are you doing cunt! I'm paying your fucking wages now sit the fuck down and don't move until I tell you to."

Mike quickly glanced in Lionel's direction and a swift nod of the head by his superior told him to do exactly as Billy said. A second later the door opened and an orderly entered carrying a tray of tea. The man eyed Billy suspiciously as he set the cups down but there was no conversation and as soon as the door closed Billy grinned wide eyed in the direction of his visitors.

"So, what's new, what you got to tell me? Is old Queenie gonna give me a pardon?"

"Sorry but not this time Mr Jackson, there is however some news to tell you."

Billy's ears pricked up and he waited with baited breath, the days here were long and mind numbing and anything out of the ordinary was a mental escape, if only for a short while.

"Well spill your guts, don't keep me hanging."

"Mr Wiseman was released from prison two days ago. His appeal was successful and the verdict overturned."

Billy instantly leapt up and began to pace the room. He wasn't agitated only pleased as he repeated the words 'son of a gun' over and over again. Finally when he'd calmed down, he returned to the table and leaning over, stared Lionel Graves directly in the eyes.

"So when's it my turn?"

Lionel had been dreading this moment and taking a deep breath he began to explain, well at least he tried to explain.

"Your situation is a bit different Mr Jackson, well actually it entirely different."

"And why pray tell is that?"

"Because Mr Wiseman was in prison, you on the other hand have been sectioned and different rules apply. Add the fact that the new evidence that allowed Mr Wisemans appeal concerned him and only him, we don't have a lot to go on."

"So what you're saying is he goes free but I'm staying in this shit hole?"

Lionel Graves didn't want to answer but also knew that he didn't have an option, he just hoped that Mike could make it to the panic button in time if the shit hit the fan. "I'm afraid that's exactly what I'm saying Mr Jackson." Billy once again jumped up and began to pace the floor, his steps quickened as he tapped his lower lip rapidly with his index finger. Mike Chapman glared in Lionel's direction as if to say 'shall I call for help?' but Lionel slowly shook his head. Suddenly Billy walked back to the table and his mood seemed to have changed as he smiled in the direction of his two visitors.

"Right you two, I've got a plan. I want you to contact Tony Smart, that's Davey's solicitor by the way, tell him to ask Davey to visit me as soon as possible. If my old friend is reluctant just say 'Southend' that should get him here. Now I think we're about finished gentleman so if you will excuse me, lunch is nearly ready and a man has to eat!"

Billy promptly left the room and the two men just stared at each other in disbelief. They had never come across the likes of Billy Jackson before and probably never would again, God willing.

At 4pm that afternoon and just after Davey had viewed and wiped the days recording the intercom in his apartment began to buzz. Davey wasn't expecting anyone and once again stared into the security monitor expecting to see another of the numerous journalists that had tried to get a story out of him. Spying Tony Smart, Davey was a bit surprised but he still pressed the button to release the main door and a few minutes later Tony stepped into the apartment for the first time.

"Nice place you've got Mr Wiseman."

"Thanks, so why are you here?"

Tony followed Davey along the hall and into the lounge. For a second the full aspect of Hyde Park from the vast windows took his breath away but he was brought back to reality when he heard Davey cough in annoyance.

"Seems Billy Jackson had....."

Davey cut the man off mid-sentence and was quickly starting to get pissed off at being disturbed for no apparent reason.

"I thought I'd already told you that I didn't want to hear that cunts name mentioned ever again?"

Tony had luckily never been on the receiving end of Davey Wiseman's wrath but he suddenly thought that might be about to change and quickly. Still, he had a message to deliver and had a sneaky suspicion that it could be important.

"Davey, please let me say what I came here to. Seems Billy is none too pleased about you getting out and he's still banged up. He asked to see you and as his team know, there's no way in hell that was ever going to happen, probably Billy knew that as well deep down. Anyway, he said to say 'Southend'."

Within a second Davey's face turned ashen and there was no need for further conversation. As Tony Smart headed towards the lift he stopped and turned for a moment.

"An appointment has been arranged for tomorrow at twelve if you feel like going to see him."

As the lift door closed Davey stood with clenched fists but there was nothing for it, he would have to go and once again that fucking faggot Billy had the upper hand.

The following lunchtime and after reluctantly driving over to Broadmoor, Davey parked the car and slowly made his way through the seemingly endless security. There was no real difference between this place and The Scrubs, they were both prisons but here you probably had less of a chance of ever getting out, well actually if your name was Billy Jackson then you had absolutely no chance. Davey was shown into the same small room that had been used a day earlier by the solicitor and his clerk and to say he was wound up was an understatement. Billy opened the door and almost leapt onto his old friend but the embrace was not returned by Davey, he stood rigid with his arms by his side.

"I knew you'd come I just knew it. Oh Davey boy it's so good to see you."

Davey was having a serious problem just being in the same room as the man and he roughly pushed Billy away.

"Did you think you could blackmail me into visiting you?"

Billy cocked his head sideways and his eyebrows were raised as if to say 'you're here aren't you?'. His expression was also one of hurt and he couldn't understand why his best friend, the only friend he had ever had in the world was now acting so cold towards him.

"I wouldn't exactly call it blackmail, I needed something to get you here and I had to use any trick in the book to see you so let's just say it was a means to an end and besides, it worked didn't it?"

"Not really, I mean yes I'm here but only to tell you that it won't work. I mean you're in the fucking Looney bin, who would the Old Bill believe you or me?"

"Why are you being like this Davey, it's not my fault what happened, the only person at fault is that bitch Fran!"

It still riled Davey when Billy bad mouthed her and even though what he was hearing was true he would never give Billy the satisfaction of being able to say 'I told you so'.

"I don't give a fuck who's to blame but you, well I was about to say my friend but there is nothing further from the truth because you ain't no fucking friend of mine! You know something Bill? You make my fucking skin crawl, have done for a long time. I'm leaving this shit hole now and I don't ever want you to contact me again. As far as Southend is concerned you can do what you like but it won't come to anything and The filth will probably be more interested in how you know so much about George Watson's disappearance. Of course you can't tell them that he's dead can you? Otherwise you'd incriminate yourself! Now fuck off and leave me alone!" With that Davey turned and walked from the room. Billy was left standing with tears streaming down his cheeks but suddenly his lips curled back into a snarl.

Shown back to the ward he was the only inmate in the room and when Ashley Little walked in and started to make fun of his tearstained face Billy lost the plot. Picking up a large, heavy hard backed book he launched it at the nurse's head with such force that it stunned the man causing him to drop to his knees. Billy then kicked out at Ashley's face rendering the nurse unconscious. Now flat on his back Ashley was in no position to defend himself and Billy was straddling the man's chest within seconds. As hard as he could Billy dug both of his thumbs into the nurse's eyes, it was a trick he'd been shown by his father years ago and with a popping sound the eyeballs jumped out of their sockets and hung down on his cheeks attached only by the optic nerve. In cases of this happening accidentally, the eye can easily be put back but Billy had no intention of allowing that to happen and when he ripped the nerve and threw the balls across the room like he was playing squash, he knew the nurse would be blind forever. Nurse Little regained consciousness and began to scream uncontrollably, the cries were high pitched and sounded like a wounded animal and it instantly alerted the other staff. The door flew open and several orderlies were soon running to his aid. Billy was unceremoniously hauled off of the man and frogmarched to a padded cell, now referred to as a room of confinement for quiet reflection. He laughed hysterically for hours as he savoured and relived in his mind this most horrendous act. Billy Jackson didn't care what happened to him now, he'd lost the love of his life and in all honesty there wasn't much more the system could throw at him. They couldn't lock him up and throw away the key as they'd already done that. If they tried physically hurting him he would enjoy it, enjoy the fact that they would have his blood on their hands and him knowing that there was a fucking good chance he'd infected them. The bastards!

CHAPTER EIGHT

A week after his telephone conversation with Jackie Silver, Gilly had been busy finalizing all of his affairs in America. He wasn't in debt to anyone but there was still all of his stuff to get rid of as he wanted to travel light and he also had to withdraw Davey's money from a security box he'd rented and somehow find a way of getting it back into England. Months earlier when Shauna had been a no-show at the airport he had boarded a plane and not really cared about anything. If the authorities had stopped him and asked question regarding why he was carrying such a large amount of cash he would have handed it over without a second thought. Now he was returning home Gilly knew it could come in handy for bribes and such but just how was he going to get it back into the country? Originally he had been set on returning the money but that wasn't the case now and he couldn't explain why but he just knew that Davey was involved somewhere along the line with Shauna's disappearance. There was still just under a hundred grand left and placing ten thousand into his suitcase he wrapped the rest in tinfoil and stuffed it into a large fur toy of a bear. Gilly didn't know if it would work but he'd once heard that the foil acted as a barrier and would block the smell of money if sniffer dogs were working at the airport.

It was a tense few hours but he couldn't believe his luck when he arrived back on British soil without a hitch and moved swiftly through passport control. It had taken him a few days to tie up the loose ends and Florida already felt like a distant memory, he also had a sneaking suspicion that however things turned out he would never ever be returning to the United States.

Deciding that it was best if he didn't reside in London, Gilly had taken a room at the Fairview Lodge bed and breakfast on Harvey Road in Guildford. It would mean just over an hour journey every time he wanted to get into London, not to mention having to tackle the M25 in part but hopefully the distance would grant him a higher level of safety. There were too many people who knew his face and associated him with Davey Wiseman to actually stay in the city and now that Davey was a free man again there would be numerous would-be gangsters desperately trying to score points and please him by offering up any information that might grant them a favour.

Edna Huggins had run her small bed and breakfast establishment for the last twenty two years and after her husband's death some seventeen months earlier, had contemplated giving it all up and retiring. The only reason that stopped her was the fact that Edna loved her home and even more she loved having guests to stay. The house was a six bedroom former Victorian rectory and was filled to capacity with, what her husband Dennis always referred to as junk. It wasn't junk to Edna, to her every single item was a memory of happy times past when the couple would go to the weekly Sunday car boot sale over at the sports ground on Nightingale Road. There was just one problem, Edna never knew when to stop buying and now the dining room overflowed to such a degree that the guests were having trouble when sitting down to breakfast. China vases, pots and fancy lace doyleys filled every surface but to Edna it was the epitome of taste. Gilly had stumbled upon the place by accident after he'd collected a hire car at Heathrow airport and had just driven with no real destination in mind as he was only looking for a one night safe haven. He had come across the house after taking a wrong turn and seeing the vacancy sign had decided it was as good a place as any to sleep for the night. Edna had welcomed him so warmly and the terms were so dirt cheap that he instantly decided it was to become his fulltime base from where to find Shauna.

On his first evening and while comfortably seated in a pub serving his favourite larger and having a bite to eat, Gilly decided that his initial port of call should be a trip to see Jackie Silver. He had to know Shauna's last movements, people she spoke to, might have written to or maybe even telephoned, in fact anything that would give him a starting point because at this moment in time he had zero information to go on. A few minutes later and after a swift phone chat the pair agreed to meet up at the cottage the following day. Just hearing the woman's voice had been a boost and returning to Fairlight Lodge Gilly slept like a baby, something that he hadn't been able to do for a long, long time. He enjoyed one of Edna's famous, well in her eyes at least, full English breakfast's before setting off. Estimating that it would be a two hour journey over to Bournemouth, by nine am he was on his way and reaching the cottage, he got out of the car and surveyed the surroundings before tentatively knocking on the front door. In a matter of seconds the door flew open and Gilly was greeted by a woman much older than he had imagined. Jackie hobbled forward and embraced him, something Gilly wasn't expecting but it was a nice friendly gesture all the same.

"Hello, you must be Gilly."

To say Jackie wore a broad grin was an understatement, she was so pleased to see him, pleased that someone was at least finally going to try and help her find her girl. Manoeuvring her walking sticks she beckoned for him to follow her through to the front room. The place was small but welcoming and for a split second Gilly had an image of Shauna sitting by the fire. She would have been so happy here and the thought scared him, there was no way she would have given this up willingly. After making tea the two sat at the dining table and for a short while there was an awkward silence until Jackie sighed heavily and eventually spoke but she was so nervous about what she was about to say. Jackie Silver never once minced her words and she wasn't about to start now, there was something that needed to be said so that the air could be cleared and after sniffing once, she began.

"I know the line of business you're in Gilly, Shauna told me all about it, all about the terrible things men like you do and I must say that under normal circumstances I would never entertain someone like you but then these are far from normal circumstances."

"Was in Mrs Silver, was in but you'll be glad to know that I'm not anymore, though whether that's a good thing or a bad I'm not really sure of at the moment because the people I will need to contact most certainly are still in that line of work."

"It's Ms and please call me Jackie. Now I really don't care what you did, do or have done to make a living in the past, all I care about is getting Shauna and the baby home safely. She was so near to her due date that the child must have arrived by now. That fact adds to my worry, she didn't attend any antenatal classes and I just pray she has had someone with her."

For a second there was more silence as they both realised there was a distinct possibility that Shauna might not even be alive. Jackie could see the concern etched onto the man's face and if he was scared then she knew her girl must really be in danger.

"I know what you're thinking Gilly, me too if I'm honest but we have to rid ourselves of such thoughts. My girl is a fighter and I prefer to think that the pair of them are safe and well somewhere. All we have to do is find them but I know that will be far easier said than done."

"Jackie, it's going to be like looking for a fucking needle in a haystack."

"So what are you saying then, you're not even going to try?"

"Of course I am, I don't think I will ever sleep again until I find out what's happened but I just want you to be aware of how difficult it's going to be if Davey has got her."

Jackie took a sip of her tea, slowly looked up and studied the man's face again before she continued. She had a gut feeling she was going to like him, Shauna already did and her girl was usually a good judge of character.

"So where do we start then?"

Gilly felt like laughing, the old girl was feisty and he imagined that years earlier she would have been a force to be reckoned with.

"We, don't start anywhere, I shall start and relay back to you anything I find out. It's a dangerous world out there Jackie and the people I used to mix with would snap your neck without giving it a second thought. I know you want to help her but the best you can do is sit tight until I

66

get in contact. It might take weeks but I'm prepared for that and I swear on the bible I won't give up until I know she's either alive or dead."

"Believe in God do you?"

Gilly laughed out loud and his reply caused Jackie to do the same.

"No not really but it sounded good."

Twenty minutes later Gilly Slade began his journey back to Guildford, the traffic was heavy and he spent the time trying to work out where the fuck to begin his search. True there were a few old faces that could possibly help him but it would be a big risk as he had learnt early on in his career that there was no such thing as honour among thieves. Just because you had known someone, had a pint or six and a laugh with them on occasion didn't mean that they wouldn't stab you in the back if it meant they could curry favour with one of the big boys. Still, when it boiled down to it he didn't have a choice in the matter and the sooner he got down to business the sooner he would see a result or at least that's what he was praying for. With the holdup in traffic it had taken nearly three hours to get back to Fairview Lodge and as he wearily stepped through the front door Edna Huggins was just coming out of the kitchen.

"Oh I'm so glad you're back Mr Slade there a letter here for you."

Instantly Gilly was in a blind panic, how could anyone know he was here? Edna handed over a plain white envelope but there wasn't anything written on it and he wore a quizzical look.

"How do you know this is for me?"

"You silly man, because it's from me Mr Slade. It's an invite for you to attend my afternoon soiree this Sunday.

67

Those morons on the committee have cancelled the car boot so I thought I would ask a few friends over for coffee and biscuits and a few of my fondant fancies. It so nice when you get to meet new people don't you think? Now I know you won't let me down and Joyce, Muriel and Stephanie have been badgering for me to introduce you to them."

"But I only arrived yesterday Mrs Huggins so how could they possibly know about me?"

"Jungle drums Mr Slade, jungle drums."

Edna was already disappearing back into the kitchen so Gilly couldn't quiz her further and he had a feeling that if these women did exist then they wouldn't have the foggiest idea who he was. Pure and simply the old girl was lonely and from his time in Florida he knew exactly what that felt like. Gilly gave a thin smile and slowly shook his head but inside he wanted to strangle the silly old bat but then in all honesty would giving up a couple of hours of his day to make an old woman happy, really matter that much? When she'd first said he had a letter his chest had gone so tight that he thought he was having a heart attack. If he'd been thinking rationally then he would have realised that there was no way anyone could know he was back, well at least not yet anyway. To calm his nerves Gilly decided that a few pints down the pub later would be called for, he had to get his act together and begin planning and he was now aware that a trip to the smoke was on the agenda for tomorrow and it was something he really wasn't looking forward to.

At just after six that evening Gilly finally decided it was time to get his arse in gear and go for that drink. Yesterday he had been reliably informed by the local paper shop owner that The Keep over on Castle Street was a good place to sup as it was quiet and served real ale, something Gilly had a fancy to try. It was situated just over a mile away so walking would be better than the risk of the Old Bill stopping him on the way back. The shopkeeper had been right, the place was great and Gilly spent most of the evening perched on a stool at the bar, chatting to regulars as if they were old friends. By closing time he was far the worse for wear and no closer to having a plan than when he'd arrived. Still, he had found out one thing, he liked the taste of real ale, the thought made him laugh out loud as he stumbled home. The mile or so journey back to the bed and breakfast would take him over an hour.

CHAPTER NINE

As he gazed out of the apartment window Davey was becoming stir crazy, the view was amazing but there could also be too much of a good thing. He was desperate to get back to work, it wasn't for the money and Lord knows he had more than he knew what to do with but he needed a distraction and what better than to make sure all of his clubs were open again and running smoothly. Now with only the odd journalist or two hanging about downstairs he knew it wouldn't be long before his appeal was forgotten about. The news was already yesterday's fish and chip papers and he couldn't deny he was relieved. Over the last week they had hounded him to such a degree that apart from The Pelican, he hadn't been able to visit any of his other clubs and Davey was well aware it was a must or the new staff, many of whom he hadn't even met yet, would start taking the piss if he didn't show his face. He also needed a new side kick, there was safety in numbers and since Gilly Slade had done a disappearing act, along with a bundle of Davey's cash, something that would need to be addressed in the not too distant future, he was on the lookout for a new employee. Anyone that had worked for Billy in the past was a definite no no and it wasn't down to the men's sexual persuasions. Davey wanted someone fresh that he could mould into his ways and suddenly it came to him, Dickie Pinter, landlord of The Black Bull over in Whitechapel. The man ran what Davey referred to a school for talent but in reality was just an easy way to employ muscle. Dickie was ex-army, corrupt ex-army and the pub was a front for anything illegal, right wing thugs being a speciality but mostly it was a place to hire bodies as and when they were needed.

At just after seven that night Davey made his way to the underground garage, got into the Jag and then drove himself over to Whitechapel. The Black Bull, situated on the High street and directly opposite the Royal London Hospital, which was handy at times when things got out of control, was a wide fronted pub but shallow in depth. Opening the front door was like stepping back in time. The place was heavily beamed and the walls were covered in green and red tartan which Davey guessed hadn't been changed since the day the pub first opened. The highly polished bar complete with brass foot rail, ran almost the entire width of the building but the place was seldom full. It was a pub for villains' and unless you were part of that fraternity you didn't venture inside, not if you knew what was good for you. In his smart suit and cashmere overcoat Davey Wiseman stood out like a sore thumb and looked oddly out of place but it only took a greeting from Dickie Pinter for him to be welcomed with open arms by everyone inside.

"Well bless my soul, if it ain't my old Mukka Davey Wiseman, you're the last person I expected to see walk through those doors. How you doing old friend? I saw you had a spot of bother but the bastards can't keep the likes of us down can they? What you drinking, scotch is it? Come on my old son take a pew. Jerry get off that fucking seat and let my pal sit down. I tell you Davey, you can't recruit an army like we used to, all too bothered about having their fucking collars felt nowadays, fucking Nancy-boys the lot of 'em. Back in our day it was a different story, men were men and right hard bastards as well, ain't that so?"

There was a spattering of mumbled moans by the

assembled drinkers but none of them had the bollocks to openly complain, well not unless they fancied a trip to the building opposite. Davey smiled as he remembered why he hadn't visited the pub in recent years, Dickie was a good sort and very old school but he also talked incessantly and in the past it had driven him up the wall. Taking a seat Davey took a large swig of the scotch that had been placed on the bar and knew he would probably neck several more before the night was out, well he would have to if he was forced to put up with Dickie for much longer.

"Can we have a word in private mate?"

"Of course we can, you should have said. As much as I try, the walls in this place still have fucking ears, mind you, if I catch any of the fuckers mouthing off they won't have any ears left by the time I've finished with them." Dickie Pinter's eyes narrowed as he slowly scanned the bar and several blokes lowered their heads rather than make eye contact with the landlord. It wasn't because they had done anything wrong but if Dickie took a dislike to you or got it into his head that you might be a bit lose with your tongue, you were liable to lose it, literally. Lifting up a small top section of the bar the landlord beckoned Davey through and showed his guest along a narrow hallway which led into a small back room that had the word 'PRIVATE' emblazed upon the door. The walls and ceiling were painted totally black and there were several small round tables placed in the room and around each were four chairs. Low pendant lights hung down on chains over each table and the landlord caught his guest eyeing up the space.

"Not much to write home about I know but we have a weekly poker night in here if you ever fancy a game. It's only been going about six months but it's well attended. Not particularly high stakes, ten grand gains you entry if you're known to us and you my friend definitely wouldn't have a problem getting in. Now what was it you came to see me about? By the way, that was a bad old result for you and Billy and I was fucking elated when you won your appeal, mind, I could never really take to Billy Jackson and not because he was a queer cunt either. The bloke was a bit of a fucking psycho if you ask me and you always had to be on your fucking guard. I can't do with geezers like that, I call a spade a spade as you well know Davey, no offence meant regarding your pal by the way."

"None taken and me and Billy Jackson are, to put it politely, estranged, very very estranged in fact. Dickie I need a right hand man, someone fresh that's trustworthy. Most of my old crew came back to work as soon as I was released but any one of them would sell their own fucking grannies if the price was right. Don't get me wrong, they're good workers but I need a side kick I can really trust to walk beside me. There's too many young guns wanting to try their luck and you need fucking eyes up your arsehole if you don't want to get done over. The bastards have no shame nowadays and it ain't safe no more unless you're carrying, which really wouldn't be a wise move for me at the moment as I have a feeling the Old Bill will be watching me like a fucking hawk."

"Say no more me old sunshine. I had a new group of squaddies' join me a couple of weeks ago, all of them had been shat on by Her Majesties government after being out on Civvy Street for a couple of months. No housing, jobs, money, fuck all in fact. No wonder half of the poor bastards turn to crime, I mean fighting for Queen and country and this is how they get rewarded? It's a crying shame really it is."

At this rate Davey knew he would be here all night and with one gulp he downed the last of his drink. Instantly Dickie stood up and walking over to an art deco sideboard, removed a new bottle of scotch and two fresh crystal glasses.

"So how vicious do you want this bloke to be exactly?" The question was short and to the point and for a second Davey was surprised into silence.

"I ain't really after anyone too heavy, but I wouldn't expect him to shy away if anyone should front up to him. Above all else Dick I need someone completely trustworthy and not liable to spill his guts for a few quid or if he got a pull by the Old Bill."

The landlord was slightly insulted by Davey's choice of words. These men were soldiers through and through and didn't shy away from anything. That said, he still understood what his old friend was trying to say.

"I think I might have just the bloke you're looking for Davey. Unlike the new batch this one came to me about a month ago and he's a bit special. Jimbo is ex Para as it goes and he's also got a right nark on with the government over how he's been treated. He's a quiet bloke and like most that pass through these doors, he takes orders well and doesn't ask any questions."

Suddenly loud voices could be heard coming from the bar and when the sound of glasses being smashed reached Dickie Pinter's ears he was out of his seat in a second.

"Excuse me for a minute Davey while I have a quick gander at what's going on, surprisingly we ain't got no CCTV in here."

Dickie laughed at his own attempt at a joke and Davey

nodded his head but stayed where he was, he couldn't afford to get into any bother so soon after winning his appeal. Dickie poked his head through the door that led into the bar and saw a young kid of no more than twenty kicking off.

"I said, I want a fucking drink! You fucking lot are a bunch of tossers', think you're hard men do you? well think again."

There was nothing to worry about as several of the men that he had previously fixed up with work soon stepped in to sort out the trouble. The kid was calling them all the low life scum in the world when one of the men stepped forward and quickly grabbed the little shits arms and forced them up behind his back. Now another of the men, a man they all knew but only as Rocky, was on his feet and he was one big mother fucker. Slowly walking over to the bar he picked up a shard of glass and proceeded to hold it against the youth's throat.

"Now then sunshine, why don't you just fuck off out of it and save us all a load of bother. This happens to be a big Boys' bar and really not for the likes of you, well not unless you want to get your head well and truly fucking kicked in."

The point of the glass shard had slightly pierced the boy's skin and he was desperately trying to stand on the tips of his toes to stop it doing any further damage.

"When my old Mukka here lets you go, I want you to walk out without a word and don't fucking think about coming back mob handed, or next time I won't be so fucking accommodating."

Rocky nodded his head and his buddy released the young scroat who instantly ran from the building to a round of clapping and cheering. Dickie made his way back to

Davey and was laughing as he entered the room.

"I tell you Davey, those fuckers know how to handle themselves and no mistake. Now where were we?"

"You were telling me about this Jimbo bloke but can I trust him Dickie, that's the question?"

"You offend me my friend. All Para's have a code and we ain't no grasses no matter how much pressure we're put under."

Davey felt a moment of guilt as he remembered the man had himself been in the Parachute Regiment and the landlord was fiercely protective of the name and all it stood for.

"Sorry Dickie I didn't mean anything by it, only I've been stabbed in the back recently and the wound is still raw."

"I heard mate, some tart grassed you up didn't she?"

Hearing Shauna referred to as a tart cut Davey to the core, if it had been six months ago then friend or no friend, there would have been serious consequences. He didn't want to feel this way, didn't want to allow her to still get under his skin but as hard as he tried these feelings just wouldn't go away. Shauna was a lot of thing but a tart definitely wasn't one of them but he thought better than to disagree with his host.

"Yeah something like that. Anyway, how much is this so called superman going to cost me?"

"Well Jimbo wants five hundred a week, which in my opinion isn't unreasonable considering what he might be asked to do and of course there will be an introduction fee for me, shall we say a grand? For that I would say you're getting a good deal as half the fuckers that come to me looking for work think they're worth their weight in gold but this time I'm confident that statement is right.

Jimbo is one of the best I've had in a long time and I can guarantee that you won't be disappointed."

Davey stood up and placed his chair neatly under the table before walking towards the door.

"That's good enough for me and thanks Dickie I owe you one. Tell him to be at The Pelican tomorrow at ten, I'll give him a few days and we'll see how it goes. I can't say fairer than that now can I?"

The two old friends shook hands and then Davey left The Black Bull slightly the worse for wear. He was concerned about being pulled over by the Old Bill but luckily that didn't happen and he was soon back in his apartment feeling better than he had in days.

CHAPTER TEN

Forget daily, Davey was now struggling every hour as he desperately fought the need to see Shauna and the baby. This wasn't him, wasn't how he reacted, he was Davey Wiseman for fuck's sake, The Davey Wiseman and he didn't allow anyone to get under his skin. Finally he decided that he couldn't take another sleepless night and pretty soon he would meet his daughter but not before he had met with his newest employee at The Pelican. At just after nine that morning Davey pushed on the entrance door and once again walked into the place that had been such a big part of his life for so long but now held little draw for him. The smell of stale beer and sweat that had never bothered him in the past as he'd always thought of it as a sign that the place was doing well, was now offensive and he wrinkled up his nose in disgust.

"Morning Boss!"

Davey nodded his head in the direction of his employee but even she now irritated him.

"Morning Janice, everything okay here?"

"It was a bit quiet last night Davey but I suppose it will take a while for people to know we're open again. I managed to get a couple of new bar people and the agency is sending someone over called Dagmar for the cleaning job. She's Polish I think, though in all honesty when I spoke to her on the blower I couldn't understand a fucking word she was saying."

"You don't need to as long as she does the job."

Janice Shackleton was a bit taken aback as this wasn't the response she had hoped for. Ever since her Alan had carried on with a Polish tart a few years ago she wouldn't give them the time of day. So what if most of them were beautiful and had figures to die for, this was her country and she would think what she liked and no one would change her opinion. Janice wasn't a bad person and deep down knew that she shouldn't tar them all with the same brush but she was hurting, still hurting after all these years and knew that she would never come to terms with her man cheating. When Davey continued to speak as he walked away, it was obvious he didn't really want to engage in conversation which hurt her.

"I've got someone coming in to see me at ten and he's a big fucker by all accounts, goes by the name of Jimbo."

"Okay Boss I'll show him through when he gets here."

With that Janice watched the man she thought the world off disappear into his office. Davey Wiseman had changed since his stint at Her Majesties and it wasn't for the better. He seemed so aloof now and there was no real banter like there used to be. Deep in thought she was staring into space when the front door again opened and a tall blond woman approached the bar.

"Hello Lady. I Dagma, I come to clean please."

Janice rolled her eyes upwards, she had a feeling that today was just going to be one of those days and she was already thinking of home. By the time she had sorted the woman out with an apron and cleaning products Janice knew she was in dire need for a coffee but that wasn't about to happen as the door swung open with such force, she wondered if the hinges were about to come off.

"Sorry love but we ain't open yet and go easy on them fucking doors will you!"

The man smiled and as he did so he revealed the most perfect set of white teeth, something Janice had always had a penchant for. He was tall, muscular and tanned and she didn't think in the whole of her life that she had ever seen a bloke so handsome.

"Sorry Sweetheart, I can see you're busy but I have a meeting with Mr Wiseman."

Manners too! Suddenly the day was turning out not to be as bad as she was expecting. Giving her sexiest smile even if she was almost old enough to be the man's mother and in her mind she used that term loosely.

"Yes of course, he's expecting you. Follow me."

Janice led the way to Davey's office and as she walked she imagined that his eyes were all over her, savouring her and wanting her. When she knocked and walked into her boss's office her face was flushed and light perspiration stood out on her brow. Davey looked up and for a second frowned.

"You okay Jan?"

"Yeah fine, I'm fine! That bloke you said about is here to see you."

James Hardy, Jimbo to his friends and associates, stepped into the office and Davey instantly knew what was wrong with his bar manager. He couldn't help but chuckle out loud and this caused Janice even further embarrassment.

"Well I have a lot of work to do so I'll leave you both to it."

Davey had never seen the woman move so fast which brought on another round of laughter.

"Think you've got a fan there, come on in and take a seat, we don't stand on ceremony in this place."

Jimbo did as he was asked and at the same time discreetly surveyed the room. It was classy with lots of highly polished mahogany and plush materials. Of course he knew of Davey Wiseman's notorious reputation, Dickie had given him the heads up in that department but as yet he knew nothing personal about the man. Jimbo was observant with a fantastic memory and seeing the opulence told him that his new boss had expensive tastes and liked the finer things in life. It was something to keep in his memory bank for later and could come in handy one day.

"So Dickie Pinter tells me you're in the market for a spot of work?"

"That's right Mr Wiseman."

"Well, tell me a bit about yourself?"

Jimbo hated this part, hated talking about a past he would rather forget but he also knew that men like Wiseman expected honesty and if he wanted to work for the man he had to be upfront about everything.

"I expect you already know that I was in the army?" The question was rhetorical so Davey only nodded his head.

"I had a bit of a shitty upbringing, actually it was fucking diabolical as it goes so the first chance I got I was out of Lewisham and didn't look back. The army is, was, my life but things turned sour about eighteen months ago. I'd just returned from a six month tour and me and four mates were on a night out. We weren't looking for trouble or anything, we'd seen enough of that to last us a lifetime in that shit hole of a place. Just a bit of downtime and a few pints you know how it is, anyway, I somehow got separated from them. We were stationed at Colchester so I decided to start walking back to base when I got set on by a couple of local blokes looking to make a name for themselves. I tell you Mr Wiseman, it pissed me off big style, I mean I'd just got used to not being shot at by fucking rag heads and here I was being set upon by my own kind. So in a nutshell, I fucking lost it and they both ended up in hospital and hurt badly.

81

I wasn't court marshalled or anything but they kicked me out of the regiment, a fucking regiment I had given the best part of fifteen years to. So, here I am and I suppose their loss is going to be your gain."

Davey liked the man's frankness and honesty. This would be a good partnership even if he would have to start training the man from the bottom.

"You'll do for me son. I expect Dickie told you a bit about what our line of work involves?"

Jimbo smiled revealing those perfect white teeth again and Davey knew that if he had any trouble with the girls at the clubs then this bloke would be able to smooth things over without a hint of violence.

"Follow me, I need to check on a few of my places. They should all be up and running again by now but it doesn't do well to be absent for too long or the cunts start taking liberties."

The two men drove over to The Royal but everything as usual was as sweet as a nut. After checking the takings and spending ten minutes with various members of staff they left. It was the same at Top To Tail but on entering The Judge's Den it was a different story altogether.

Stepping into the main entrance Frieda Cousins could be heard shrieking at the top of her voice and it was something Davey didn't like to hear but knew that it wouldn't be happening without good reason.

"Why you little bitch! Come back here and say that to my face, come on I fucking dare you."

The group of woman who had congregated to see the showdown suddenly parted and a young girl of no more than twenty swaggered over. With the support of her work mates she now had courage and a big amount of attitude, which didn't bode well with her manager.

82

"Me and the girls have been talking and we're all fed up to the back teeth with you ripping us off Frieda. Me and them want a bigger cut, after all its our fucking fannies that take a pounding from those dirty cunts every night and not yours. Mind you I shouldn't think your flange has seen any action for years!"

The brasses all laughed which made the older woman see red. Frieda swiftly lunged forward and grabbing a handful of hair pulled down sharply. The young girl was helpless and down on the dirty carpet in seconds.

Without hesitation Frieda swung her leg and with the toe of her shoe swiftly kicked out several time with as much force as she could muster. Her aim was on target and she made contact with her victim's ribs. A piercing scream rung out in the foyer and Jimbo was about to step forward but was instantly stopped when Davey barred the way with his arm.

"It's best not to get involved when Frieda's on a mission son. She's been managing my girls for years and knows what she's doing."

Davey's words were spoken with sincerity, he knew the woman wasn't vicious unless it was called for. Frieda Cousins was always extremely careful not to mark the girls in a way that would be overly visible to a punter but all the same, punishment had to be dished out at times to keep them all in line.

Amy Kimber had only been on the game for a few weeks but had already been making waves and causing upset amongst the other brasses on a daily basis. The problem stemmed from the fact that when Amy had arrived on a train from up north she had, like many before her, thought that the streets would be paved with gold.

The truth couldn't have been more different, brasses were ten a penny in London, especially if you were unlucky enough to be lower down the scale in the looks department which Amy definitely was. Now the girl, who only seconds earlier had acted as if she had more balls than the proverbial pawn shop, was silenced. With her skirt around her waist leaving little to the imagination, the young woman lay on the ground clutching at her sides and instantly the rest of the girls had disappeared without comment. There were no morals or loyalty when you were on the game, not if you wanted to continue working in a place that was relatively safe. The Den was seedy and held little charm but Frieda Cousins, as hard as she was, did care about her toms and always tried to make sure that they were treated right by the clients.

"Frieda? What the hell is going on here girl, it sounds like a fucking fish wives convention?"

In a trance like state, it took a couple of seconds for it to register with the woman that she was being spoken to but looking up, she smiled when she saw Davey.

"Hello Mr Wiseman, I didn't see you there. That silly little sod has been mouthing off again and stirring up trouble. Now I don't mind her winding the others up as it's nothing I can't handle. One look from me and the other leery cows normally shut their traps in an instant but what I do take umbrage with is when she starts moaning to the fucking punters. Trade is thin enough on the ground as it is at the moment and the last thing we need is for the punters to start feeling sorry for the whores, I tell you Mr Wiseman, this place will be the death of me one day, it really will."

Frieda quickly cast her gaze over her boss's companion

and her eyes were instantly out on stalks which made Davey laugh again.

"Frieda, meet Jimbo. He's now my right hand man and is taking over from where that cunt Gilly Slade left off."

"Well hello! Ain't you a sight for sore eyes pretty boy and definitely a lot easier on the eye than Gilly was. Not that I ever really took to the back stabbing little bastard." Frieda bent down to retrieve her shoe that had flown off during the altercation.

"So how you doing Mr Wiseman, world treating you well?"

Davey laughed out loud, this place never ceased to amaze him. Everyone who worked here was completely off of their trolleys and if you'd written down what happened here no one would ever have believed you.

"I'm good thanks love. Come on Jimbo we have work to do."

The two men once again set off on their travels but never in his wildest dreams, would the newest addition to the Wiseman empire have been able to imagine what he was about to learn regarding his new boss.

CHAPTER ELEVEN

Shauna was starting to go stir crazy locked up in the basement and it had nothing to do with JJ or the baby blues, the child was an angel and motherhood was a breeze because of it. What Shauna craved was adult conversation, there were only so many cooing and gurgling sounds a person could put up with in a day let alone hearing them twenty four seven. She guessed it was fine weather outside as the basement was hot and humid and the damp smell had diminished, oh how she longed to feel the sun on her face, not to mention the fact that it couldn't be any good for the baby being cooped up down here. The Russian was still bringing food daily, or at least Shauna thought he was Russian or from some other eastern bloc country. The man had only ever said to her 'eat' or 'no talking' so she hadn't been able to judge too much from his accent. He looked mean and never smiled unlike Ray, oh how she missed Ray, he'd been so kind to her and she hoped he was safe and hadn't gotten into any trouble for helping her.

After leaving Top to Tail Davey and Jimbo had set off for the farmhouse but it would turn out to be a very long journey. Instead of heading straight for Bournemouth Davey insisted that Jimbo drive to Croydon then on to Reading, Basingstoke and Guildford before finally heading to their destination. Instead of the hundred mile trip it had turned out to be double as Davey's Jag zig-zagged from town to town in an attempt to avoid anyone that might be following him, especially the Old Bill. He needn't have worried as the coast was clear. As much as he would have liked to, Neil Maddock had bigger things

to worry about at the moment and tailing Davey
Wiseman, was at the bottom of his list. Still, Davey
wasn't taking any chances and when they pulled up at the
house around five thirty that evening both men were glad
that they had finally arrived. Jimbo was told he could
stretch his legs for a few minutes and then instructed to
get back in the car and stay there. He was under no
circumstances to enter the house unless anyone turned up
unexpectedly. Davey cast his eyes over the front of the
building and then opening the front door he could feel his
stomach begin to churn with nerves, something he
definitely wasn't used to feeling. It had been months
since he'd last set eyes on Fran, he corrected himself,
Shauna, he was never going to get used to her real name
but it wasn't just that, he was about to meet his child,
well the only one he was aware of and considering she
had been conceived in love, well on his part at least, he
was scared shitless. Davey had been given the exact
location of where she was being held so he walked along
the hallway to the back of the staircase and stopped at the
basement door. The keys were hanging on a hook by the
frame and after two attempts he finally managed to open
the four padlocks and slid the heavy bolt across. As the
door creaked open he was hit by the stench of the
unwashed and he wrinkled his nose in distaste. The noise
of someone entering scared Shauna and she clutched JJ to
her breast. The days food rations had been brought in
hours ago so there should be no one else coming until
morning and she prayed that whoever it was, they were
here to help rather than to harm her. Davey nervously
took the first few steps down into the basement and when
he set eyes on Shauna his heart instantly flipped. She had
did the best she could to wash but her hair still hung

greasy and lank upon her shoulders, her clothes were dirty and even though she'd recently given birth she had definitely lost weight. None of that mattered to him, to Davey she was as beautiful as ever. Shauna gasped when she saw who it was and quickly standing up from the old armchair she held onto JJ tightly as fear that he was here to take her baby engulfed her. The two just stared at each other in silence and Shauna could feel her hands tremble, not wanting to scare JJ she somehow summoned up the courage to speak.

"Hello Davey, I knew you'd come sooner or later."

"Did you now?"

She smiled weakly but he didn't return the greeting. Images of his incarceration fleetingly filled his mind and out of nowhere he was suddenly filled with anger. For a moment he couldn't speak, didn't want to speak to a woman who he had loved and who had cold heartedly stabbed him in the back in the worst way imaginable. It felt as if his hard steel-like stare was boring through her very soul. She knew how vicious and cruel he could be and in all honesty she couldn't blame him if he had come to kill her, his love for her had probably died the day that she betrayed him.

"Please tell me you haven't come to take her away Davey? I couldn't carry on if I lost her."

His lips curled back as he spoke and his words were said with such spite and venom that she took a step back in fear.

"If I had then it wouldn't be any less than you fucking deserve Fran but what would I do with a fucking kid?"

"You know my name isn't Fran and just in case you're interested, I named your daughter Jacqueline, I call her JJ

88

for short."

Shauna slowly took a few tentative steps forward and approached the man who only a few months earlier she had sent to prison, a man she both loved and hated in equal measure.

"Meet your daughter Davey, JJ this is your daddy." Holding the baby away from her she waited for Davey to take the child, strangely he did and as JJ looked upwards and gurgled, his heart instantly melted.

"She looks just like me!"

"Yes she does, I can also see Vonny in her. My sister had the same curly hair when she was a baby."

The mention of Vonny stunned Davey for a second and he searched Shauna's face for any sign that she was reminding him of what he'd done. There was nothing, it was purely a reference to someone else that had been precious to her. Standing in the basement gazing down at their daughter together felt so cosy and right but as much as he wanted to tell her everything would be okay and they could pick up where they had left off, he couldn't. She had to pay, they always had to pay, it had been the ethos he'd lived by for his entire adult life and he wasn't about to change that now. Abruptly he pushed JJ towards her mother and as she took the baby Shauna stared at him with pleading eyes.

"Don't you dare fucking look at me like that. Did you really think this could ever turn out well?"

"Of course I didn't Davey but I hoped it....."

Davey had no intention of letting her finish and cut Shauna off mid-sentence.

"Sit down and listen. I have a suggestion, no let me rephrase that as it's not a suggestion it's how things are going to fucking be and you have no say in the matter.

89

I'm going to buy a house for you and the kid."

"Oh Davey that sounds wonderful I..."

"Not so fast, I haven't fucking finished yet! You will live there and raise my child. Neither of you will ever want for a thing but you will never, ever be allowed to leave."

"What you mean is that we'll be prisoners?"

Davey paced around the small area that had become Shauna's home and he fingered a few of the baby items as he spoke.

"That's exactly what I mean, you will be a prisoner just like you tried to make me. If you try and escape I will take the baby and you will never see her again. Do you understand?"

Shauna could only stare in horror at what she was hearing.

"I said! Do you fucking understand?!!!"

His voice was raised and aggressive, something he had never been with her before, well at least not in her adult life.

"Yes I understand and thank you."

"For what?"

"For not killing me because I know Billy Jackson would've."

Davey's eyes narrowed as he slowly shook his head, pursed his lips and without another word he climbed the stairs and relocked the basement door behind him.

Outside he walked slowly around the building not wanting to get back in the car while the stench still penetrated his nostrils. Taking a few deep breaths he had to place his hand on the brickwork to steady himself.

This wasn't how he thought it would be, wasn't what he wanted it to be either. On arrival he had hoped that he wouldn't feel anything, that he would be able to hurt her, maybe the baby as well but all he had felt was love and it scared him. Davey got into the car and sat in silence.

"Are you ready to go Mr Wiseman?"

When Davey didn't reply Jimbo was unsure if he should ask again. He hadn't known the man five minutes and from what he'd heard from Dickie Pinter, Davey could be a right nasty bastard if he had a mind to. Dickie had instructed him to do everything he was told without question and to never get under his boss's skin or rub him up the wrong way. The two men must have sat in silence for at least five minutes and then out of nowhere Davey spoke.

"Get me back to the smoke and don't take the long way." Jimbo started the engine and drove at speed. They were making good time until they merged onto the M25 and the traffic was soon at a standstill.

"We would probably have been better to have taken the long route Mr Wiseman."

Jimbo's attempt at humour fell on deaf ears, Davey was in a bad mood and the glare he gave Jimbo was enough to tell the man to keep his mouth shut. When they hadn't moved for almost twenty minutes Jimbo switched off the engine and got out of the car. In the distance he could see several flashing blue lights and knew there must have been a pretty bad accident.

"I don't think we'll be going anywhere soon Boss, looks like there's been a right pile up a bit further on."

Davey didn't reply and only continued to stare ahead as his mind went in to overdrive thinking about Shauna and the baby. It was dark by the time they at last reached London and Jimbo was instructed to drive straight to the apartment. Davey got out and the only words he spoke was to tell the man to collect him at ten the following morning. Jimbo wasn't exactly sure what to do with the car so he decided to have a drive about and see what was going on in the West End. Dickie Pinter had given him the heads up on Davey's clubs and now that he had actually seen them for himself he fancied taking another look when they were running at full speed. Pulling up outside The Royal Jimbo was stopped by the two doormen. They recognised the Jag but not the man, when he explained who he was and who he worked for the door was instantly held open but he didn't stay more than a few minutes as the place was too stylish and Jimbo liked things seedy, in fact the seedier the better though looking at this Adonis no one would ever have imagined that. Giving Top to Tail a miss he headed straight for The Judge's Den and as he entered was greeted warmly by Frieda.

"Hello handsome, twice in one day I am truly honoured." Watching him devour the girls with his eyes, Frieda knew exactly why he was here. She found it strange that someone so gorgeous, who could have his pick of beautiful women, would prefer to spend his time with brasses.

"Jimbo, can I ask a question? Why on earth would you want a tom when you could probably have any woman that took your fancy?"

He smiled showing those perfect white teeth again but unlike before, Frieda now saw something that sent a shiver down her spine but she couldn't for the life of her explain what it was.

"Because I don't want to waste my time wining and dining a bird just to get a quick fuck now do I? I'd rather pay and be on my way, so which one of the dirty whores is available."

Frieda pointed in the direction of Amy Kimber, the young girl who had given her aggro earlier. If he was as twisted as she thought he might be then it was maybe time for a little payback. Clicking her fingers she motioned for the girl to join them and when Amy saw who her next punter was she grinned from ear to ear. Normally sex meant nothing to her and she shut down until the deed was done and the trick had paid up but this time things might be a little different. Taking hold of Jimbo's hand she led him through the club and out into the rear yard. The barrel store was partially covered and would give them a little shelter.

"Lift up your skirt and bend over."

"My, you're a fast mover but then I like a man who knows what he wants."

Amy did as she was asked and waited for him to enter her but she wasn't expecting what happened next. Jimbo clamped a hand over her mouth and then roughly pulling her legs apart slammed his erect penis into her rectum. Amy screamed out in agony but the sound was muffled, she tried desperately to bite at his palm but it was useless and with every thrust she felt as if her insides were being ripped apart. Tears streamed down her face and she prayed to God for it to be over, her prayers must have been answered as a few moments later he was spent and releasing his hand he zipped up his flies and casually but somewhat arrogantly, strolled back into the club. Amy had fallen to the ground and a cocktail of blood, semen and excrement was now slowly seeping from her back passage. Her legs felt like jelly and her heart was racing as she tried to stand but it was as if every bit of strength she possessed had deserted her and the pain was so intense that she knew he had damaged her badly.

Her whole body began to tremble as she curled up into a foetal position, desperate for the agony to stop. As Jimbo walked through the foyer in the direction of the main door Frieda stood watching and when she realised that Amy hadn't come back she went looking for the girl. The outside lighting was dim and reaching the yard she couldn't see anything but suddenly a whimpering sound guided her towards the barrel store. Seeing Amy's position Frieda knew exactly what had happened as she too had suffered the same fate many years ago and kneeling on the floor she took Amy into her arms.

"Oh dear Lord whatever has he done to you sweetheart? Come on darlin' let old Frieda give you a cuddle."

Amy was a kid, albeit a mouthy one but still just a kid and Frieda may have wanted the young brass brought down a peg or two but never would she wish something like this on any of her girls.

"He's a dirty, sadistic bastard my love but he'll get what's coming you mark my words."

Davey would hear about this, new minder or not, no one damaged his girls without his say so. They would now be one tom down for weeks because of Jimbo's actions and Frieda knew her boss wasn't going to be too pleased about it.

CHAPTER TWELVE

Whilst Gilly's replacement was in the throes of carrying out his vile act, Gilly had spent the last hour and a bit on his mobile trying to contact anyone he thought he could trust not to run back to Davey Wiseman. Mental Dennis, Ron the Fence and Leroy Lee were just a few of the names whose numbers were still stored in his phone but they had all drawn a blank. At just after eleven that night his luck changed when as a last resort he had dialled Ray Harvey's number. The two had shared several pints over the years whenever Barry McCann was doing business for Davey. It had never been on a very personal note but there was still something Gilly had liked about Ray, he couldn't put his finger on what it was but even though they were both in the same line of work, which was sometimes very unsavoury, the man seemed an honest sort and not the type liable to shaft you without reason. Ray and his wife had decided on an early night and were in bed when the phone started to ring. The noise woke Sally who then prodded her husband but there was no response. Ray was snoring loudly but it didn't deter her and using her index finger she poke him sharply in the ribs making him jump up.

"What the!!! What the fuck are you doing woman?"

"Your mobile's ringing Ray now for fucks sake answer it before you wake up the whole bleedin' house! Those kids have school in the morning and will be a bloody nightmare to get ready if they don't get enough sleep."

"Alright, alright! Don't fucking go on Sal."

Grabbing his phone from the bedside cabinet he swiped the screen but didn't speak until he was out on the landing and the bedroom door was firmly closed. Not having looked at the mobile he didn't have a clue who was calling this late, he was just desperate to stop the incessant sound of Freddie Mercury singing 'We will rock you', a ring tone he usually liked but not at this time of the night with an irate wife giving him daggers.

"Yeah?"

"Hi Ray it's Gilly, Gilly Slade."

For a moment Ray was lost for words and slowly descending the stairs, made his way into the kitchen. Flicking on the kettle he took a seat at the table and began to chew on his bottom lip. Ray knew about all that had gone down between Gilly Slade and Davey Wiseman, or at least he was aware of the rumours. He also knew that the man had scarpered and rightly so if he wanted to continue breathing, so why was he calling Ray? Well there was only one way to find out so taking a deep breath he spoke.

"Hell old son, how you doing?"

"Not too bad thanks but you've probably guessed I ain't calling to ask how your day has been. Any chance we can meet up pal, you know I wouldn't ask if it wasn't an emergency."

Ray thought for a moment, if Barry found out he would have Ray's guts for garters but at the same time Ray knew what it felt like to be in trouble and have no one to turn to. He was taking a chance but Gilly was a good sort and he wouldn't be asking if he wasn't desperate.

"Of course we can, when and where?"

Without giving away his location Gilly explained that he would rather stay away from London so the two agreed to meet the following lunchtime at the entrance to Chessington Zoo. At fifteen miles outside of London it was exactly half way in distance for them both although Ray wasn't privy to that fact. Returning to bed, his wife rolled over and groggily asked who had called.

"No one you'd know, now gimme a kiss wench I've got a right storker on."

Sally giggled and duly obliged much to the pleasure of her husband.

It was no such luck for Gilly and he lay awake for hours worrying what the morning would bring. He must have dozed off eventually but it didn't feel like he'd had any sleep when the alarm suddenly decided to burst into life at seven thirty. After a leisurely breakfast and an inane conversation with Edna Huggins just to kill some time, Gilly finally set off for his meeting. Chessington Zoo was busy with coach loads of school children and it took several minutes before he was able to find a parking space. The two men had agreed to meet at the main entrance and a nervous Ray was already there when Gilly approached. Seeing Gilly glance around every few seconds as he walked towards him put Ray further on edge but he still held out his hand as soon as the man was standing in front of him.

"How you doing Gilly, long time no see."

"I'm alright mate thanks. Shall we grab a coffee?"

Gilly went to pay the entrance fee but when they saw it was thirty nine pounds each they just looked at each other. It was beyond steep and even though there was always safety in numbers they both looked across the road at a burger van that had parked up at the verge on the off chance of getting some passing trade.

"Come on Gilly let's go over there, I ain't gonna let you pay all that just to get a fucking coffee."

Drinks sorted the two men then climbed into the front of

Ray's very old Mondeo just as the rain started to come down. To begin with the conversation was stilted, Ray knew that he was probably going to be asked to reveal information he wasn't happy to and Gilly was struggling with how to begin asking questions that just might help him find Shauna.

"Family alright?"

"Yeah fine thanks, though my eldest is a right fucking pain in the arse, teenagers hey?"

"Too true Ray, I wouldn't want to go through all that bollocks again. We had it good in our day but it's not like that for kids nowadays."

The men laughed but it was forced and they were both aware that sooner or later one of them would have to begin with the reason why they were here. It would be a miracle if Ray could tell Gilly anything about Shauna but he at least had to try, if he drew a blank then he really hadn't got the foggiest idea where to turn to next.

"I don't suppose you know why I wanted to meet up but just let me explain before you knock me back and tell me to get the fuck out of your motor. You're probably aware I left London under a cloud, you've also probably heard that I stabbed that piece of shit Wiseman in the back?"

Gilly waited for a response but Ray only stared at him waiting for him to continue.

"We both know that in our game nothing is ever as clear cut as it seems, the trouble is that people only listen to the version from the bigger fish. Well I was just a fucking tiddler so no one was interested in my side of things. That's all irrelevant now and you probably haven't got a fucking clue what I'm talking about but in all honesty mate you're my last fucking resort."

"Thanks for that!"

"No, I didn't mean it like that, it's just I've tried every contact I know and the majority didn't even want to speak to me, the others, well let's just say if they did know anything then the cunts weren't fucking sharing it. I reckon Davey already knows I'm back by now that's why time is of the essence. There was a woman......"

"Ain't there always?"

"No seriously Ray, hear me out. This is deadly fucking serious, and I mean deadly. Shauna was a kind sort and didn't deserve what I assume Davey has.........."

"Shauna!"

Gilly's heart skipped a beat when he realised the man knew exactly who he was talking about.

"You know her?"

Ray's face went as white as a sheet and he suddenly wished he was back at home and had never agreed to this meeting. His expression didn't go unnoticed but Gilly wasn't about to let up.

"Ray? Come on mate, if you know anything you've got to tell me! She's disappeared and I think he's going to kill her, the poor little cow is pregnant as well."

"You mean she was pregnant!"

Gilly felt nausea wash over him. He could go in heavy handed as Ray wasn't really any match but if he was ever going to get information that was any use to him then he had to tread carefully.

"Look mate, I can tell you a few things but not much."

"Anything, anything at all might be a help Ray, I just need to find out..."

Suddenly like a bolt of lightning it hit Ray Harvey. Gilly was in love with the woman.

"Is that what this is all about, you fucked Davey Wiseman's bird?"

99

"What? No, no I didn't! Do I love her? Well yes I suppose I do but that's as far as it ever went I can assure you."

For a few seconds Ray pondered what to do. This could open up a whole can of fucking worms and he didn't know if he was prepared for that but at the same time, could he live with himself if he just left the woman to her own fate? Ray knew the answer but he still had to be careful and not reveal anything that might put Sally or the kids in danger.

"Okay. Now what I tell you is never to be repeated and when I've finished I don't want you pushing for more because there won't be anymore, do you understand?"

Gilly vigorously nodded his head, he couldn't believe that at last he might actually be onto something.

"All I can tell you is she's had the kid and the two of them are doing fine, or at least they were the last time I saw them which was a little over a week ago now. She is being held in a house and before you ask, no I ain't revealing its location."

"But I...."

"Fuck! Gilly I told you, don't put pressure on me or you can fuck off out of it right now."

Ray waited for Gilly to interrupt again but when he didn't utter a word Ray continued.

"I reckon she's been there for a good few weeks, they might well have moved her by now but even if they haven't, it would be more than my fucking life is worth to tell you where she is. Barry's already on my back and if I shaft him over this then who knows what would happen. As much as I liked the girlie, I have my own family to think about in all of this. If you want my opinion for what it's worth, then I don't think the fucking outlook is rosy for her but what can I do? Now that's as much as I'm willing to say, so if you don't mind I have work to do."

Gilly stepped from the car just as Ray started up the engine but before he drove away he lowered the side window.

"I don't have to tell you to be fucking careful Gilly, this is personal and when its personal men do weird fucking things. I wish you well my friend but please don't contact me again."

Ray Harvey sped off leaving Gilly standing alone in the pouring rain and not having a clue what to do next. For his own safety he had purposely stayed out of London but now it looked as if he wasn't going to have a choice in the matter.

Returning to the guest house he gave his notice to Edna and then packed what little belongings he had. After a bit of research Gilly then drove over to Enfield, Avis had a rental place on Grove Park where he would be able to return the car. It was getting expensive and in any case there was no need for him to drive in the city. Public transport could get him where he wanted to go much easier and quicker, there was also the added fact that he could instantly disappear down one of the tube stations if he was spotted by anyone. His ex-sister-in-law still lived on the Rowley Way estate in Camden Town and Gilly knew she would always put him up for a few nights. Jumping on a Northern line train he didn't have to change and nine stops and just over twenty minutes later he emerged from the bustling station onto the High Street. The smells and copious amounts of people suddenly made Gilly realise how much he had missed the place.

True, there were so many foreigners that half the time you couldn't hear a London accent but it was still the only place Gilly Slade had ever called or ever would call home.

The Alexandra and Ainsworth Estate, affectionately known by the locals as Rowley Way, was a council estate completed in nineteen seventy eight. Entirely built of reinforced concrete it housed five hundred and twenty flats over a varying design of four and eight storey buildings. With its overhanging terraces and numerous walkways it was soon the chosen location for many film and television series and strangely, to Gilly at least, it had now been given a grade two listing meaning its blot on the landscape would remain forever more. Linda Slade lived in flat two eighteen, she'd been married to Gilly's brother back in the early eighties but when the union fell apart after Stevie Slade had run off with a neighbour, Linda had remained living alone on Rowley Way. Gilly rang the doorbell and prayed his sister-in-law was home and luckily for him the door was opened almost instantly.

"Well bless my soul, if it ain't my wayward brother-in-law."

Linda stepped to one side and as Gilly passed her she poked her head out of the door and looked from left to right to make sure no one had clocked who her visitor was. In the small rear kitchen Linda leaned with her back against the sink and studied her visitors face.

"So, to what do I owe this honour?"

"I need a place to stay for a bit."

Linda laughed mockingly as she slowly shook her head.

"You've got a bleedin' nerve, I had this place turned over a few months back. Two blokes, none too fucking friendly I might add, came looking for you and wouldn't take my word that you weren't here. Anyway, from what I've heard you ain't short of a bob or two so why not a hotel?"

Gilly sighed heavily, this was going to be more difficult than he'd first thought. His normally lovely sister-in-law was now showing more than a tad of animosity towards him but then again, as he looked around at the flat which she always kept in pristine condition, he could see why she would be pissed off with two of Davey's men coming in and trashing the place.

"Because dear Linda, I need to stay under the radar. Now obviously I will bung you a few quid, so can I fucking stay or not?"

Linda Slade walked past him and into the hallway but just before disappearing into the front room she spoke.

"Okay, but I promise you this, if you bring any fucking aggravation to my door there will be bleedin' murders and I don't mean from the henchman of that wanker Wiseman!"

Gilly clenched his fist in euphoria, he was back and now he could really get started in his quest to find Shauna.

CHAPTER THIRTEEN

The day after he had been to see Shauna, Davey visited five Estate Agents in his local area. After stating what he was looking for he was shown several properties but nothing had been suitable. What he had in mind needed to be detached, in a quiet area and most importantly, far enough away from any other building so that any neighbours wouldn't become suspicious. Deciding it was time to cast his net a little further he had Jimbo drive him over to Welwyn Garden City. It was thirty miles out of the Capital but still close enough for him to visit whenever the mood took him. Davey had a little knowledge of the area but not enough for him to decide where to buy a house, so telling Jimbo to stop the car on Parkway, he got out and walked down Howardsgate and into Garden Estate Agents. The three room shop was void of any other customers and within seconds he was approached by a salesman who was eager to boost his monthly commission. Davey explained that he wanted to purchase a nice quiet retreat for his aging parents. The agent, Gavin Withers, was the typical stereotype of his trade and as arrogant and overconfident as any estate agent could be. When he clocked Davey's sharp suit and cashmere overcoat, he knew his salary was about to escalate and place him in prime position for the deal of the month award.

"And may I ask what Sir's budget would be?"

Davey already loathed the man, was it any wonder people hated estate agents with twats like this working in the trade.

"Sir has, as you so eloquently put it, no budget as such, it just has to be the right property."

104

All Gavin could see were pound signs in front of his eyes
and quickly walking over to a filing cabinet he removed
three or four sets of details. Shuffling the papers into
order he motioned for Davey to take a seat.
"Now here are a selection and I have put them in order
starting with the best."
"Don't you mean the most expensive?"
"Sorry Sir, I don't understand?"
The question was rhetorical but when Davey flicked
through the list, it wasn't the most expensive that caught
his eye.
"I'll take a look at this one."
"Good choice Sir! That's a very good choice indeed, if
you don't mind me saying."
Davey didn't reply and strolled out of the office with
Gavin Withers following in hot pursuit. Burnham Green
was four miles from Welwyn and Davey didn't think
he'd ever been to anywhere more beautiful. Passing
fields and hedges he couldn't help himself when he saw a
sign for Robbery Bottom lane, that one would have
tickled Billy and for a second he found himself thinking
of his old friend. Gavin's car pulled up in front of a large
set of wooden gates and the Jag stopped and waited
behind while the agent opened up. A large granite plaque
on the wall read 'Journeys End Defiant' which intrigued
Davey. They approached down a long drive that was
densely filled with pine trees before the house at last
came into view and Davey knew instantly this was the
place he was after. Gavin hurriedly unlocked the front
door but after a quick look around Davey had seen
enough much to the disappointment of the agent.
Stepping back out into the sunshine Davey spotted a man
pushing a wheelbarrow on the other side of the vast lawn.

About to walk over he was stopped when Gavin grabbed his arm and again started his sales patter.

"For fucks sake Jimbo, shut the cunt up before I do him some real damage."

James Hardy instantly had the estate agent by the throat and was pushing him up against the wall as Davey continued on his way. The man who Davey took to be the gardener let go of the wheelbarrow handles, removed his flat cap and began to rub at his sweaty head.

"Nice day?"

Davey held out his hand and the man readily accepted and at the same time introduced himself.

"Henry Shadbolt but everyone just calls me Shadbolt. I'm the gardener, been here for over twenty years, you buying the place then?"

Davey smiled, the old boy seemed friendly enough and he supposed it was a fair enough question.

"I'm considering it, why?"

"No real reason, I just thought it would be nice to see someone living in the old place again. It's been empty for over a year now and things have started to deteriorate."

This was music to Davey Wiseman's ears and he would now be in a position to negotiate hard.

"Old Mrs Roache loved this place, you know she used to feed the squirrels from her hand, mind she could be a feisty old bugger if the mood took her, I've had the sharp end of her tongue many a time. Spent most of her days reviewing books and would write her remarks in the margins in Latin, could never understand a word myself but she was a nice old girl all the same."

"What happened to her?"

"What Mrs Roache? She died the poor love. Right out

of the blue it was, mind you she was ninety eight and none of us can go on forever can we?"

Davey had to fight to hold the laughter inside as he slowly nodded his head in a show of understanding and respect.

"No Shadbolt I guess we can't, anyway, what's with the name of this place?"

Shadbolt grinned and Davey could swear he almost saw the old timer's chest swell. The gardener liked nothing more than to give his advice or answer questions and this was a story he loved telling, though most of the locals were already aware of it by now.

"Molly, that's Mrs Roache to you, well she travelled all around the world with her husband. Travelled for years she did on account of The Captain being in charge of a liner. You know I don't think I ever knew his real name as she always referred to him as just The Captain, anyway, when he was about to retire Molly found this place and told anyone who was happy to listen that she was never moving again. And you know something? She never did, hence the name 'Journeys End Defiant'. You ain't going to change the name, are you mister?"

Davey placed his hand onto Shadbolt's arm and assured the man that wouldn't happen.

"I think it's a fine name Shadbolt and it would be a crying shame to change it after all these years."

Walking back over to Jimbo who had at last released the agent from his grip, he smiled and informed the man that he would take the property and wanted a speedy sale. He also told Gavin that his offer would be fifty thousand below the asking price. Gavin's face lit up and he instantly forgot about the unpleasant experience of a few moments ago.

"That's wonderful Mr Wiseman and between you and me, I have inside information that the figure will be acceptable to the late owner's estate. May I ask if a mortgage is required?"

"Nosy little cunt ain't you, no it isn't."

"Well then I'm sure we can have you moved in within a few weeks."

As Davey spun around with a furrowed brow, Gavin Withers instantly realised that the man, if provoked, could possibly be as vicious as his employee.

"Oh no sunshine, I'm having it next fucking week or you'll have to answer for the delay personally and I can assure you that it won't be nice."

"But Sir there are legal searches to be done and those wheels turn very slowly which is out of my control."

"Just you sort out your end and leave mine to me. Jimbo get the car!"

Just as Davey said, the sale went through seven days later with the legal works set to be carried out after completion. Jimbo picked up the keys to 'Journeys End Defiant' from Gavin Withers and informed the man that Shadbolt the gardener would no longer be required.

"But I was under the impression or at least Mr Shadbolt was under the impression, that he would remain working as a gardener at the property for the new owner?"

Jimbo only had to take a step forward for Gavin to hold up the palm of his hand in surrender. Memories of his last meeting with the man were still fresh in his mind and he didn't want a repeat performance, especially here in front of the office girls. With the keys in his possession Jimbo then did as he'd been instructed and made his way over to Whitechapel and The Black Bull.

On entering the pub he instantly noticed how quiet it was, which for a public house situated in the middle of North London, was unusual to say the least, he also knew better than to ask questions about things that didn't concern him. Dickie Pinter was sitting at the bar reading a daily tabloid when the door opened and on seeing who it was, he smiled from ear to ear.

"Well bless my soul! Hello Jimbo mate, nice to see you, how's life treating you?"

"Fine thanks Mr Pinter, I'm really liking the work. Nice to see you're rushed off your feet today!"

Dickie ignored the last remark.

"Glad to hear it my son, so what can I do for you?"

"Not me actually, Mr Wiseman sent me. He needs some bodies to do building work on a property he's just bought. He said he didn't want anyone knowing it's for him and that's why he sent me to see you."

"Understandable, so what's he need then?"

Jimbo handed over a detailed drawing and on inspection Dickie puffed out his cheeks.

"Well whoever's going to be living there won't be getting out in a hurry that's for sure, still, no business of mine. Tell your Guvnor it's best if we use foreigners, they're cheaper and don't ask questions. A while back I had three or four Polish do some work on this place and they certainly know their stuff, mind you they can be right moody cunts, wouldn't want to cross them if you know what I mean? So what's it like working for the notorious Davey Wiseman? Bet you've seen a few things that would make Joe public's hair curl in the short time you've been in his employ, although in all honesty I have to speak as I find and I ain't ever had a beef with the man, pays on time and is about as fucking trustworthy as

109

they get in this game."

Jimbo was surprised at how quickly he'd forgotten that Dickie had verbal diarrhoea and he was now wondering if that was the real reason Davey had sent him rather than coming himself.

"Well I'd best get back to the club Mr Pinter, nice seeing you again."

"You too and tell the big man I'll be in touch as soon as everything's set up. Stay safe."

Before the front door had closed Dickie Pinter was already on the blower to a contact he knew. Kuba Kaminski was one of the few eastern Europeans that Dickie would allow to drink in The Black Bull. The man spoke reasonable English and didn't have an attitude like so many of the others, that and the fact that he was a fantastic tradesman allowed him entry into a place that normally had the reputation of being a closed club. In reality Kuba didn't care much for Dickie or his regulars. He found them to have a chip on their Shoulder's about having foreigners in their country but it didn't deter him from making the effort to stop by once a week for a few beers. The work he gained from his weekly visits was well worth having to tolerate these people for an hour or two. By noon that day Kuba had arrived and was shocked when he was shown the plans.

"I know what you're thinking Kuba but it's nothing to do with us. The labour rate will be double what you usually get but I need your best men and they have to be trustworthy and able to keep their fucking traps shut."

"Of course Mr Pinter, so who is the job for?"

"Sorry I can't say, it's strictly on a need to know basis I'm afraid. I will be paying your wages and the only person you will have any contact with, so how long to complete it?"

"Let's say a week, ten days at the most. You know my men Mr Pinter, they don't pussy around."

"Yeah good blokes I admit, shame the lazy cunts around here don't fucking work as hard but then they're all on the fucking dole and know they can get good money for sitting on their arse's and the rest are mostly Pakis. No offence mate but foreigners come to this neck of the woods for a free fucking ride."

"None taken Mr Pinter, you have free speech in this country and can say what you like."

The two shook hands on the deal and when he was once more alone Dickie tapped Davey's number into his phone.

"All sorted, ten days' time and that place will be like fucking Fort Knox."

There was no reply and the line went dead without a thank you or goodbye. Nine days later Kuba Kaminski had completed the task before the given schedule. As Davey walked from room to room he was impressed with the workmanship, everything was falling into place and very soon he would have her and the baby just where he wanted.

CHAPTER FOURTEEN

After his meeting with Ray Harvey, Gilly had continued to phone around in the desperate attempt to find someone else that could help him. With every knock back he received he was growing increasingly angry until he finally snapped. There was nothing for it, he would have to put more pressure on Ray and hopefully by going to see him on his home turf and also in his local The Ace, would do just that. Hopping on a train he emerged from Edmonton station. The trip had been over ground as there were no tubes this far out and he hadn't wanted to do the two and a half mile walk from Tottenham Hale as it would have been too risky. Approaching the pub Gilly had a spring in his step as he opened the front door.

"Sorry mate, we ain't open yet. Why don't you come back in half an hour?"

Gilly walked over to a grey haired man who was kneeling on the floor and trying without success to wire in an electrical socket but who in fact would have looked more at home dishing out a good slap.

"There are professionals for that you know."

The man didn't reply and carried on with what he was trying to do. His attitude didn't bother Gilly, it was the same in any of these places and something he'd gotten used to over the years.

"Anyway, I ain't here for a drink pal. I actually wanted a word with Ray Harvey, is he about?"

"Sorry mate but you're out of luck on that score 'cause the lazy cunt ain't turned up yet. No telling what time he'll show his ugly boat, want to leave a message for him?"

It was obvious that the man's words were an attempt at

politely telling Gilly to get lost and not wanting to draw any undue attention he walked back in the direction of the street door.

"Just tell him Gilly was here to see him will you?"

Gilly slipped out onto the road but not before he had been glimpsed by Barry McCann. Emerging from the gents toilets and doing up his flies as he walked, he wasn't quite sure if his eyes had deceived him.

"Who was that Dano?"

"Some twat looking for Ray apparently but I ask you, who has a

fucking name like Gilly?"

Dano's words instantly had Barry staring with his mouth wide open.

"What's up, you look like you've seen a fucking ghost or something."

Barry didn't reply and walking back into the bar knew he had a real dilemma on his hands. Should he keep his trap shut but then the shit might really hit the fan, on the other hand if he fessed up to Davey there was no telling what would happen. Deep down Barry knew it wasn't really a dilemma as in this game it was all about self-preservation not matter what the cost and to whom.

Davey had just entered The Pelican when the bar phone started to ring and as Janice hadn't arrived yet he was the only one on hand to answer.

"Yeah?"

"Is that you Davey? Its Frieda, I've been trying to get hold of you for a couple of days but every time I call that cow Janice says you ain't there."

"Well maybe I haven't been Frieda, now, tell me, what the problem is and keep it short as I'm busy."

Frieda proceeded to reveal in detail all that Jimbo had

done to Amy Kimber but Davey didn't bat an eyelid, at least he didn't until it was explained to him that the young girl was so damaged she wouldn't be able to work for a good couple of weeks at least.

"Leave it with me Frieda and I'll get it sorted."

"But he's hurt her bad Davey and I ....."

"For fucks sake! I said I'll sort it and I will."

With that he slammed down the receiver and marched into his office just as his mobile decided to ring which annoyed him further.

"For fucks sake will I ever get any peace! Yeah?"

"Mr Wiseman its Barry McCann, seems an old employee of yours was here a few minutes ago looking for my man Ray. Gilly Slade?"

Just the mention of Gilly's name made Davey see red but that was the least of his concerns, Ray Harvey had been helping to take care of Shauna, what if he'd given Gilly the location?

"You what!!! I want you to find the cunt, I need to know if he's spilled his guts."

"And then what Mr Wiseman?"

"Silence the cunt forever! I'm sick to the back teeth with every fucking low life knowing my business do you here?!"

"But he's got a missus and kids Mr Wiseman and old Ray ain't a bad
bloke as it goes."

This was turning into a bitch of a day but Davey knew he had to stay calm as the last thing he needed was for people to start thinking he was losing his touch.

"Barry."

"Yes Mr Wiseman?"

"Does my reputation precede me?"

114

"Sorry Mr Wiseman but you've lost me?"

"Am I, in your humble opinion, a right nasty cunt and think long and hard before you answer."

"Well yes Mr Wiseman, that obviously goes without saying but I...."

Barry McCann could feel his legs as they started to buckle and he had to take a seat on the bar stool to stop from falling over. Men like Wiseman didn't make idle threats and Barry now wished he'd never made the call. The trouble was, he had and now it was time to step up to the plate if he wanted to survive the day.

"Sorry Mr Wiseman, of course you are Mr Wiseman."

"Let me know what you get out of him Barry and limit the people involved in this."

With that the line went dead and Barry placed his mobile down onto the counter top. Tapping a drum roll onto the bar with his fingers he desperately tried to think of what to do next. This was going to live with him forever but he had Hobson's choice in the matter so calling Igors' number he told the man to go and collect Ray from his home and drive him over to the lockup. The men were to wait until he arrived as he had a job for them to do.

Barry then called Ray and it took all of his resolve to act naturally as he spoke to the man.

"Hi Ray, Igors' is coming to pick you up. I want you to drive over to Ardra Road and wait for me as I have some work for you both to do."

Hanging up Ray turned to his wife and laughingly said 'Hallelujah we can eat this week'.

At The Pelican Davey was pacing the floor like a cat on a hot tin roof as he waited for news even though he knew it could take quite a while. When the office door opened and Jimbo walked in Davey spun around on his heels and the man bore the full force of his frustration.

"Where the fuck do you get off hurting one of my girls you sick sadistic cunt?!!!!!"

It was now Jimbo's turn to be nervous. He hadn't thought that the old hag at The Judge's Den would really grass him up but she had and now he was in deep trouble. True he was more than capable of taking on Davey Wiseman, well physically at least. He could beat the man to a pulp without any real effort but he also needed work and the fact that he would forever be looking over his shoulder if he lashed out at a known face stopped him retaliating.

"Look, I apologise Mr Wiseman, things just got a little out of hand. You know how it is when you get a hard on?"

Davey stormed over towards the man and stopped so close that Jimbo could feel his boss's breath on his cheek as Davey spoke. The man's eyes were like steel and fine spittle escaped his mouth with every venomous word, something Davey had learned to do very early on in his career when he'd realised that it instilled fear in even the hardest of men.

"Know how it fucking is? You almost ripped the arse out of that poor little cow, how is that getting 'a little' out of fucking hand? You are one lucky cunt today because if I didn't have so much other aggro to deal with then I would probably sort this out in a fucking entirely different way! You really make me sick, well I'll tell you this for nothing, the money I lose because she can't work, is coming out of your bastard wages! Now get out of my fucking sight!"

Barry McCann kept a lock up on Ardra Road for just such an occasion as this but in reality it had never been used for anything violent, it hadn't actually been used for anything at all. Back when he'd first started out in this game, which was more years ago than he cared to remember, he had dreams of being a serious player, a man that people looked up to, a man that was revered. Purchasing the small warehouse that sat alongside Deepham's sewage works had made Barry feel like he was in the big league but in reality he never progressed any further than fetching and carrying for some of the bigger named firms. Until recently when he'd branched out into small time armed robbery he hadn't warranted having his own workforce but nonetheless he had still paid out weekly for men he didn't need but who made him feel like he was important. Well things were certainly about to change on that front but if the truth be told, he wished that they weren't.

Just before Igors arrived at Ray's house, Barry had called him and told him what was about to go down but the Russian didn't breath a word to Ray. Igors Petrov hated the English, in fact, he hated anyone that wasn't Russian and was only in this country for the money he could earn and to avoid the warrant that was out for his arrest back in his homeland.

Inside the lockup Ray Harvey was having a nose about at the far end and he turned sharply when Barry McCann stepped through the small door that was inserted into the roller shutter. Ray didn't know why but he suddenly had a bad feeling that things weren't all that they should be and as he walked forward he was stopped by Igors who was now holding a steel baseball bat.

"What's going on Mr McCann? What's all this about?"

"Oh Raymond, Raymond, Raymond, what the fuck have you been up to son?"

"I don't know what you mean Mr McCann, I ain't done anything that I shouldn't have. Come on Mr McCann, you're scaring me shitless now."

Barry wasn't enjoying this one bit, he hated violence which was an oddity in his line of work but he knew he had to do as he'd been told and see it through. It was true he'd carried out unsavoury tasks for Davey and Billy Jackson in the past but he had always instructed one of his men to do the hurting. Barry now wanted this over with as soon as possible so to move things along he mentioned just two words and waited for Ray's response.

"Gilly Slade!"

The colour instantly drained from Ray's face and he knew he was in deep trouble but he worked for the man and Igors, as much as he was a cunt, surely he wouldn't do any real damage to a workmate?

"I can explain Barry, honestly it's nothing. Gilly came to see me asking about the girl but I didn't tell him anything. He thinks I know something but I wouldn't tell him, that's all it was honest to God."

Barry slowly walked around the small unit that in a past life had been used as a mechanics workshop, as he did so he was wondering what to do next. Finally he removed his mobile and called Davey Wiseman's number. The stress was doing his head in but luckily the phone only rang twice before it was answered.

"Hi Mr Wiseman, Barry here. I did what you asked and Ray didn't breath a word, said that Gilly asked him a lot of questions but he kept his trap firmly shut. So is that it then?"

Davey couldn't believe what he was hearing, was he

dealing with a bunch of retards?

"Is the bastard still breathing?"

"Well yes Mr Wiseman but I..........."

"Shut the fuck up! Now I don't care how you fucking do it but shut that cunt up permanently and cut his fucking tongue out for good measure."

"But he's got a family Mr Wiseman?"

"He should have thought of that before he got involved in my fucking business. Now I need to send out a warning to anyone else who might be thinking about poking their fucking noses into things that don't concern them. As for that cunt having family, so have you Barry so fucking think on and do as I tell you! Oh, and I ain't too happy with that Russian cunt either, I saw what he did to Shauna."

"What do you mean?"

"He knows, so tell him to be on his fucking guard as well!"

The call came to an abrupt end and with a quick nod in Igors direction, Barry turned and headed swiftly out of the lockup. He heard the first scream as he closed the door behind him and the pitiful sound saw him bolt towards his car.

Inside the unit blood was already flowing and Ray had felt his front teeth shoot out of his mouth with the first swipe of the bat. Strangely the pain was minimal but then again, he was so scared that his endorphins had probably kicked in making him numb to any hurt, at least for the moment. Now on his hands and knees he pleaded with the Russian but his slurred words fell on deaf ears and it wasn't because Igors couldn't understand the plea but purely down to the fact that he was enjoying the

119

sensation of inflicting pain. With every contact the bat made, skin and bone flew out and within a few seconds the beating had become so ferocious that Ray Harvey was no longer recognisable, not that anyone would ever be asked to identify him. After today he would simply disappear from the face of the earth. Sally Harvey would spend the rest of her life in turmoil wondering where he husband was but she knew the circles he mixed and worked in, knew that these men were capable of anything so she didn't ask too many questions. A monthly envelope would be placed in her letterbox and Sally knew to remain silent, her kids had lost one parent and they couldn't afford to lose the other. When he was sure Ray was dead and the bloody bubbles escaping from his mouth was merely the last of any oxygen left in Ray's body, Igors opened up the old inspection pit situated in the centre of the room and rolled Ray's corpse into it. He was tired to the point of exhaustion but had enough strength left for one last task. Igors always carried a bag of builders lime in the back of the van and removing it he threw the contents liberally over the body. After replacing the boards and washing down the concrete floor, no one would ever know what had occurred inside only minutes earlier.

CHAPTER FIFTEEN

Sitting in his office at The Pelican, Davey mulled over all that had happened and what action he had to take next. He was also well aware that moving Shauna was now paramount if he wanted to stay out of prison. Things were spiralling out of control, too many people knew his private business, something that would have been unheard of in the past and that realisation made him think of Billy and how tight they had been over the years. They had shared nothing with the men that worked for them, preferring only to discuss anything work related with each other. Davey had broken the rule of a lifetime when he'd allowed Gilly and Shauna into business talks and he had to admit that Billy had been right, if he hadn't have trusted them none of this would ever have happened and Billy would still be free, though whether that was a good thing or a bad he wasn't exactly sure. What he did know was that if Gilly Slade ever found her there was no telling what would happen. There was no way Davey would ever risk losing her again and then there was his baby, the only child that had ever pulled at his heart strings. He had to get things moving but he had very few people at his disposal, well not anyone he could trust and he still wasn't a hundred percent sure about this Jimbo bloke. The man had come across as sound to begin with but after the incident at The Judge's Den, Davey now had grave doubts that James Hardy was going to fit into his organisation. Suddenly he missed Billy, missed being able to pick up the phone and talk to his old Mukka, because at the end of the day, Billy might have been a psychotic little faggot but the one great thing about the man was that he always had and always would have

Davey's back covered. It was pointless even thinking about things that weren't an option and he knew that when it came down to it, contacting Barry McCann was his only choice so reluctantly he called Barry's number. There was no warm greeting or asking about the man's health, instead Davey got straight down to business.

"I need you to do something."

"Hello Mr Wiseman, didn't think I'd hear from you so soon."

Davey gritted his teeth, it was no wonder Barry had never amounted to being little more than a street criminal. It was an unspoken rule that you hardly ever mentioned anyone's name in a call just in case the line was bugged and Davey had known plenty of past associates who were now indefinitely banged up because someone had been loose with their tongue.

"Move her on Friday."

"And just how do you want me to do it Mr........"

Davey instantly lost his cool and as he spoke his tone was irate and fine spittle now covered his handset.

"For fucks sake you thick cunt, will you stop using my name!"

"Sorry Mr, I mean yes of course sorry I didn't think."

"You never think you twat and that's the reason you'll never be a face. Now listen, I want it done in the early hours, less traffic and nosy cunts to notice what's going on. Tell that monkey of yours to be gentle with her but not to engage in any chit chat. Let me know when it's done and there had better not be any problems or I will hold you personally responsible, do you hear me?"

Barry began to blab away and it took several seconds before he realised that the line was dead and he was talking to himself. Barry McCann then blew out his cheeks in an over exaggerated manner. Igors had been beside him throughout the conversation and he hoped his sidekick hadn't heard what was being said or the crawling manner in which he'd spoke but he had and Igors was now toying with the idea of moving up a scale. Maybe this Davey bloke needed some muscle and would have some work for him, after getting rid of Ray Harvey he had realised that this was his vocation, he liked violence, liked dishing it out and the sooner he tasted blood again the better. As usual, the following day Igors was sent to deliver Shauna's food and at the same time he informed her that she would be leaving the basement in two days. Shauna, much to her own surprise, clasped her hands together and actually jumped for joy. It wasn't anything to do with seeing Davey but purely down to the fact that at long last she would be getting JJ out of this rat infested hovel. The night before she was due to leave she had managed, with limited amenities, to give herself a good wash and all of the baby's things had been neatly packed, though she imagined that Davey, if true to his word, would have everything brand new in the place he was moving her to. It was strange but she wanted to keep all the things that she already had, they were now precious and had been with her child since JJ was only a few days old.

Unexpectedly to Shauna, the move was made in the early hours of the morning, very early in fact. She was still asleep on the camp bed and when the basement door slowly creaked open she shot up with a racing heart. The single burning light bulb that had been continually switched on since her incarceration was dim and with tired eyes and when the bright light of a torch was shone directly into her face she tried to shield her eyes with the back of her hand. Shaking with fear she glanced over to where JJ was and then her eyes darted back to the person standing in front of her. He was tall and thickly set but with the torch held at head height and still glaring into her eyes she couldn't see his face.

"Who are you, what do you want?"

"Get baby, we go now."

Recognising his voice Shauna now knew that it was the man who brought her daily food. A man that had always looked at her in a strange and frightening way and she prayed that he was really here on Davey's behalf and not to do her harm, which could also have been Davey's plan. Shauna had resigned herself to the fact that somewhere along the line she would have to pay for what she had done to him and maybe this was his sick revenge, maybe he'd changed his mind about placing her and JJ into a house. Igors had been given strict instructions and whereas before he had never had any physical contact with the woman, well except for the incident when he'd pulled her hair, an action he now deeply regretted after Barry had warned him of Davey's words, he gently helped Shauna to her feet.

"Come now, get up."

"What time is it?"

"Four am."

"Where are you taking me?"

"I do not know, must wait for instructions. Come now we must hurry."

With JJ clasped tightly to her breast Shauna slowly and unsteadily climbed the basement steps and once outside, when the cool night air filled her lungs, she began to sob with relief. Never had she imagined that fresh air could feel so good and she wanted to savour the moment but Igors took hold of her elbow and guided her towards the side door of a people carrier.

"What about all my things, the baby's things?"

"No time, we must leave now."

Not wanting to antagonise the man, when he slid open the door Shauna cautiously stepped inside. The windows had been blacked out but then she hadn't thought it would be any different, the one thing she did hope for was not being moved to another windowless room. Hearing a mobile ring she tried to strain her ears but it was no use she couldn't hear what was being said but obviously it concerned her. With trepidation she sat back in the seat, she would just have to wait and see what happened. It didn't take her long to realise that not only were the windows blacked out so no one could see in, they had also been coated on the inside so that she couldn't see out, not oncoming traffic, illuminated houses, not one thing that allowed her to feel normal. In the pitch dark the engine sounded so much louder and every bump and pothole somehow felt exaggerated and once again the anxiety began to build up until she wanted to scream. Knowing that it wouldn't have helped in anyway Shauna clenched her jaws until the unease at last passed.

The journey took just over two hours and by the time they arrived at Journeys End Defiant Shauna was exhausted. JJ had been grizzly for most of the journey and having no sleep herself Shauna just wanted to lie down for a while. Igors quickly open the door and the early morning sunshine seemed to fill the inside of the people carrier. The only sound was that of bird song and again Shauna prayed that she wasn't about to be put into a darkened room. Glancing all around at the trees and space she sighed to herself, it really was stunning but what the inside was like was another matter. Shauna took a few steps in the direction of the large lawn but she hadn't gotten more than a couple of metres before her arm was firmly gripped.

"No! You go in house, now!"

His tone was once again menacing and the fear and dread of what he might be capable of filled her entire body. Not wanting to exasperate the situation further she did as she was told. Shauna followed him to the front door where Igors removed a key and after opening up, gestured with his hand for her to go inside. As soon as they had both entered he locked the door behind him and at the sound Shauna felt all the anxiety she had experienced in the basement return with a vengeance.

"Now what?"

"You live here simple!"

Walking from room to room Shauna couldn't believe how big the place was. Plush carpets covered every floor and the house had been furnished with good taste but then Davey always was the epitome of good taste when it came to his standard of living.

"I go now."

Shauna spun around and suddenly she didn't want to be alone, didn't care who was here with her as long as it was someone, anyone, she just craved the contact of another human being.

"Why? Where are you going?"

Igors Petrov didn't reply and walking towards the front door he unlocked it and stepped outside. As the heavy wood slammed shut Shauna ran over and began to beat with her hands as hard as she could. Tears streamed down her face but she didn't scream or shout but very softly she pleaded 'please don't leave me'. After Igors locked the door he was about to get into the car when he suddenly stopped, he hadn't checked everywhere like he'd been told to do. Walking all around the property he scanned the windows and tried all of the other doors. In his mind he was thinking that the Polacks had been working here and you couldn't trust them to do anything properly. Satisfied that everything was as it should be Igors got into the carrier and without looking back, drove off.

Shauna was watching from the front window and as he disappeared down the drive and out of view she suddenly realised that there were bars on the window. Not ugly bars exactly, they were very ornate like the kind you saw on villas in Spain but she was in no doubt that they had been put in place to stop her getting out rather than to stop anyone getting in. Laying JJ, who was now sleeping soundly, down onto the floor, Shauna ran from room to room but it was the same at every window. She began to panic when she realised that the railings had been placed so close to the glass she wasn't even able to open any of the windows. Running into the kitchen she hysterically pulled opened every drawer and cupboard frantically emptying the contents out onto the tiled floor but there was nothing that could be used to try and prise her way out. Davey had thought of everything, even the cooking utensils were made of plastic, knives, forks, everything she would need had been provided but not one item was made of metal. Running up the stairs she searched for a loft hatch, maybe she could get up into the roof and break a few tiles, someone at least might see her or hear her. At the top of the landing she saw it and her heart was racing as she slowly climbed up onto the banister. Balancing precariously she almost lost her footing but quickly put her hand out onto the wall to steady herself. Shauna pushed upwards with as much force as she could muster but the hatch wouldn't budge. It had been screwed shut and as she climbed back down onto the landing the realisation hit her that she was once more a prisoner only this time she could see outside, see the trees and the grass but couldn't feel them. In a strange way this was worse than the basement, at least there she wouldn't be tormented but then maybe that was what he wanted, maybe he was trying to send her crazy.

CHAPTER SIXTEEN

Gilly had been holed up in his sister-in-law's flat for several days now, and to her he seemed to have lost the will to live. Linda had never been known for her patience and she was getting fed up with him hanging around. She didn't mind him bunking down here at night but she liked her own space during the day. Ever since Stevie had left her she did what she pleased and didn't answer to anyone. Now all of a sudden here she was having to cater to someone else, consider their needs rather than just her own and it was starting to get right up her nose. Finally when she went to watch her morning programme, a daily ritual she really enjoyed and not only because she had the hot's for Phillip Schofield, she found Gilly sprawled out on the sofa engrossed in a film. A dirty cup and plate sat untidily on the coffee table but when she saw a chocolate bar wrapper lying on her pure white sofa Linda snapped.

"So how much longer are you planning on being here?" Gilly was a little taken aback with her tone. It was obvious he had pissed her off but he didn't know why as he'd bunged her a ton earlier in the week so it couldn't be anything to do with money. Maybe it was her time of the month, he knew women usually got a bit leery when they were on the blob although he would have thought his sister-in-law was well passed that stage of her life.

"Well thanks a bunch Linda and who exactly has shit in your path?"

His words hit home and she realised she wasn't being fair, selfish maybe but definitely not fair. Gilly wasn't a bad man, in truth if she'd been a few years younger she knew he would have been a far better match for her than his brother had been.

"I'm sorry Gilly, that was rude of me. I'm just so used to being on my own and having you here, well to be honest it rubs me up the wrong way. It's nothing that you've done, well not really, Oh I don't know maybe I'm just set in my ways, just getting bleedin' old I guess!"

"Ok Sis if that's how you feel. I get the message, so a week, two at the most and I'll be out of your hair. What say I make us both a brew?"

Linda smiled and nodded her head, she supposed she could manage for a fortnight as long as that was all it would be. Gilly gently squeezed her shoulder and winked as he passed her on his way to the kitchen. Waiting for the kettle to boil he couldn't help but think how much precious time he was wasting. The only problem was, he really didn't have a clue regarding what to do next. There had been no news since Ray Harvey's revelation and he hadn't heard back from the man since calling in at The Ace. Finally deciding that things had gone on long enough he grabbed his jacket from the back of the chair and headed out of the door, Linda would just have to wait for a cup of tea. Making his way over to Edmonton he walked into The Ace looking as though he didn't have a care in the world, though nothing was further from the truth. Inwardly he was shaking but he had to show a front to anyone watching that he wasn't in any fear of the place. Barry McCann was as usual seated at the bar and he almost choked on his beer when he saw Gilly enter.

"You've got a fucking nerve you cunt! I bet Davey Wiseman don't know you're here?"

Gilly ignored Barry's question, it was rhetorical and if it wasn't meant to be then the bloke was a lot thicker than

Gilly thought.

"Where's Ray?"

The question and the mention of Ray's name instantly filled Barry with guilt but he couldn't admit to the feeling and instead he just shrugged his shoulders, a gesture that told Gilly even if he knew he wasn't about to share the information.

"Why don't you just do one and do us all a fucking favour you back stabbing cunt! Davey told me what you did and to a top geezer who treated you like his own, you're lucky my blokes ain't here or they'd kick seven bells of shit out of you."

"Leave it out McCann, you ain't got any fucking blokes unless you're referring to those couple of tossers' you pay to hang around. You really are a sad bastard, did you know that you were always a standing joke between Davey and Billy Jackson? They used to have a right laugh about you wanting to be a real player unlike the fucking toy gangster that you are."

Barry's mouth hung open and not wanting to get into a deeper argument Gilly turned and walked out of the pub. There was only one thing for it, he would have to pay a visit to Ray's home. Normally that would have been a taboo in their line of work but desperate times called for desperate measures. Walking along Hertford Road he wracked his brains trying to remember where exactly Ray Harvey lived. Suddenly it came to him when he recalled years earlier having gone to a party at the man's house and that it was on Wellington Avenue. He just hoped that the Harvey's still resided there. He couldn't remember the exact number but knew it was a corner property that backed onto some allotments. Ray had told him in a fit of giggles when they were half cut that he hadn't paid for a vegetable since the day he'd moved in. Turning into the avenue Gilly could see that the area was run down like a lot of the other housing in Edmonton. Everywhere looked much the same but a few minutes later a row of terraces came into view. Choosing the end house on the right he was relieved when after just one knock, Sally Harvey answered.

"Hello girl, I don't suppose you remember me but I'm a pal of your Ray's. Gilly, Gilly Slade and I was wondering if he was at home love?"

Gilly wished he hadn't opened his mouth when Sally suddenly burst into a flood of tears. He hated to see a woman cry and pulling her to him Gilly gently patted her on the back.

"Come on now sweetheart, things can't be as bad as all that."

Sally sniffed loudly and between sobs managed to explain what the problem was.

"Oh yes they can! My Ray ain't been home in two days, in all the years we've been together he's never done that, well not unless he got himself banged up and I just know something's wrong. Not so much as a bloody phone call and that bastard Barry McCann won't tell me anything, he just says he ain't seen him but I know different. I'm worried sick I am, I can't sleep and its hard trying to hide it from the kids. I can't go to the Old Bill, well I could but I have the kids to think about and besides my Ray would never thank me for it. What do you think has happened Mr Slade?"

Gilly had a sneaking suspicion that he knew exactly what had occurred but he was in no doubt that he wasn't about to share that thought.

"I ain't got a clue Sally love but I'm sure he'll be home

with his tail between his legs before long. Now you take care and if I see him I'll tell him to get his arse home pronto so you can read him the riot act. Now are you sure you'll be okay?"

Sally Harvey wiped her eyes, sniffed loudly and then took a step back in embarrassment. She didn't know what had come over her, she was usually shy with strangers but when the man had mentioned Ray's name it was as if all of the worry had just spilled out.

"I will be once he gets home and God help him when he walks through that door!"

Gilly couldn't help but smile as he turned to walk away.

"Well I'm glad it's him and not me, take care love,"

Now deciding to take a trip back to Bournemouth to pay Jackie a visit, he hoped there was the slightest chance that she might have forgotten something, any little thing that might give him a clue to Shauna's whereabouts. Gilly knew it was clutching at straws but straws were about all he had at the moment and anything was worth a punt. Taking a train as Shauna had several months earlier, it somehow made him feel closer to her as he gazed out of the window at all of the countryside just like she must have done. His mind wandered back to the day that he had seen her off at the station and it felt like years ago. By the time he reached Bournemouth and then made his way to the cottage it was just after five and Gilly felt drained. He hoped that there would be the offer of a bed as he really didn't fancy travelling back tonight but as he approached the house he had a thought, what if Jackie Silver wasn't home, what if she'd gone away or something and this trip had all been for nothing. That didn't turn out to be the case and as soon as she opened the door she greeted him like an old friend.

133

"Hello! Come, come on in and I'll put the kettle on. Where's your car?"

Gilly followed the older woman along the hall and into the kitchen and Jackie didn't stop talking. He noticed that she still wasn't too good on her old pins and probably didn't get out much, all of this must have been playing havoc with her health.

"I came by train as I've moved back to London."

Jackie busied herself but as she gathered cups from the cupboard and placed the kettle onto the hob she still continued to talk.

"So what's the news, I take it you have come here with some news?"

He'd been dreading the question and as soon as she asked it he sighed heavily, making Jackie spin around.

"What, what is it? She isn't   "

"No of course she isn't! Well at least not as far as I know but in all honesty I've not managed to find out much. I mean, I know Davey has her that's for sure but where he has her I haven't got the foggiest. I did find a bloke that knew and I was working on him but now he's strangely disappeared."

Jackie sat down at the small kitchen table with a heavy thud and rested her walking stick up against the wall.

"Well that's convenient!"

"Not for him it ain't as I now think he's probably dead, actually I'd put money on it."

"Oh my God! The poor, poor man!"

"I'm afraid that's the world I was mixed up in and the kind of world that Shauna came to know as well."

"So what now?"

"I really don't know Jackie. I was hoping that maybe there might be something you'd forgotten, anything you can remember happening while she was still here that might have been a little out of the ordinary?"

Jackie shook her head and at the same time wiped a tear from her cheek. What on earth was it with Gilly and women today, this was the second one who had shed a tear in front of him.

"Everything with Shauna was always out of the ordinary, that's what made her so special. I'm sorry, I just miss her so much and I'm so worried about her and that poor little baby."

Gilly gently smiled.

"Well on that note I do have some news, seems she had a little girl but that's all I know."

Suddenly it was all too much and Jackie began to sob, she cried until she didn't have any tears left. Gilly didn't say a word, not until the woman wiped her eyes with the back of her hand and then took a sip from her china cup.

Staring hard into Gilly's eyes Jackie wasn't sure how he was going to take her next sentence but nonetheless it had to be said.

"I think it's about time you went to the police."

"The Old Bill! You've got to be fucking kidding ain't you? I might be a lot of things Jackie but a snitch I ain't."

"Well then Mr Slade I really don't know where we go from here and if your loyalties lie with your gangster friends rather than with Shauna, I suppose there's nothing more to be said on the matter is there?"

Her words hit home and it didn't take Gilly more than a few seconds to respond.

"They aren't my friends and put like that I guess you're right. You know, Shauna always said you were a wise old bird."

135

"My girl was a good judge Mr Slade and not so much of the old thank you very much."

"Our girl Jackie, our girl."

"Would you like to stay the night?"

Gilly smiled and at the same time gently touched the back of Jackie's hand with his palm.

"I thought you'd never ask."

"It's Shauna's room and the bed is all made up, I usually turn in about eight my old legs have just about given up by then but you stay up as long as you like. Now let me fix us some supper and we'll talk some more about our girl and her baby."

True to her word, that night Jackie was tucked up in bed by eight and due to it having been a long day, well emotionally at least, Gilly wasn't much later. As he lay in Shauna's bed with the soft sheets touching his skin he imagined that he could smell her, smell her perfume and it made him feel closer to her than he'd ever felt before. As he drifted off to sleep he whispered under his breath 'I will find you and bring you home sweetheart, I promise'.

CHAPTER SEVENTEEN

The following morning Gilly warmly kissed Jackie Silver on the cheek, climbed into a taxi and made his way to the station. The train journey back to London was very different from the one on his arrival. Since Jackie's suggestion yesterday regarding him going to the police he hadn't been able to think of anything else. There wasn't one single part of the idea that didn't go against the grain and he just couldn't imagine walking into a police station voluntarily, let alone asking for the help of a copper. It was fourteen minutes past one when the train finally pulled into South Hampstead station and as Gilly stepped onto the platform it felt as if a huge grey cloud was hovering above his head. The city, a city he had always loved now seemed harsh and unwelcoming. He didn't really want to go back to Linda's flat but he had nowhere else to go so after catching a tube to Camden he soon found himself walking along Rowley Way. Treading the long red brick-weave lanes that seemed to go on for an age he glanced up at the concrete flats and even the ones that had been purchased and were now private homes with balconies festooned with tropical plants, seemed cold and oppressive. He wondered why his sister-in-law hadn't taken up her right to buy back in the eighties, she was only telling him the other day that a two bed flat like she had was up for close on a half a million but hindsight was a wonderful thing and sometimes a person wasn't meant to have an easy life. Poor old Linda would probably see out her days here as a tenant but Gilly was certain that wouldn't be the case for him. After seeing the beauty of Bournemouth and tasting the fresh air he wanted out of the city as soon as possible and hopefully he would be taking Shauna and the baby with him if he could just find her.

Suddenly he knew what he had to do and turning around he walked back out of the estate. It was a fair old trot but forty minutes later and Gilly was almost at his destination but as he approached Agar Street police station he could feel the knot begin to tighten in the pit of his stomach. It took several attempts but he finally swallowed hard and pushed the entry buzzer on the highly polished brass plate of the door. Once inside the first thing he noticed was the odour of authority, in reality it was just the smell of disinfectant from an earlier clean up when one of the local winos had decided to defecate where he stood in order to get arrested and gain a bed for the day. Walking up to the counter which was protected by toughened glass, he spoke into a small mesh screen in the direction of a non-uniformed receptionist. The woman slowly looked up from her paperwork and smiled at him which took Gilly by surprise.

"Is it possible to have a quick word with Detective Neil Maddock?"

"If you would like to take a seat Sir I will speak to my sergeant for you. Who should I say is calling and what is it regarding?"

"Just tell him Peter Slade sweetheart, he'll know who it is."

Gilly did as he was asked but he wasn't happy at being so exposed and knowing that anyone could just walk in off of the street and recognise him. Someone who would most likely know his old boss, or at least an associate and after clocking him would go running off with the information.

138

Neil Maddock was as deep into the on-going case as he could be without raising any suspicion. Since Davey Wisemans release his mind could think of nothing else and he was desperate to nail the bastard. It was almost as if it was a personal quest, no not almost, it was and deep down Neil knew it but he just wouldn't or couldn't be honest with himself. The white collar fraud case was boring and predictable but would definitely result in a prison sentence. The only problem was the fact that there had been no blood and guts, nothing for Maddock to really get his teeth into and take his mind off of Wiseman. Edmund Pearce, Manager of the City Bank over on Canary Wharf, had been laundering money and had spilled his guts as soon as he'd been arrested, now it was just a matter of rounding up the others involved and it would be case closed. Neil was about to take a break when a call from the duty sergeant saw him speechless for a few seconds. He was very aware of who Peter Slade was although he was more used to hearing the name Gilly rather than Peter. It could only mean one thing, somewhere along the line Wiseman must be involved.

"Tell him I'll be right down and whatever you do, don't let him leave!"

Neil descended the stairs two at a time and the inner doors flew open as he bounded in. Gilly had been getting more and more uptight which was heightened when he saw a couple of the brasses from The Judge's Den brought in. He knew that if they clocked him they would leak word onto the street that he was grassing someone up but in all honesty the women were too bothered about having their collars felt than to show any interest in a man they may or may not remember from one of the clubs.

"You wanted a word? What can I do for you?"

Noticing Gilly's eyes as they darted in every direction DCI Maddock could instantly read the man's mind, he'd been in the company of enough criminals over the course of his career to know the signs.

"Would you rather we talked in private?"

Gilly gave the slightest nod of his head but it was enough for the detective to walk towards one of the side interview rooms while at the same time motioning for Gilly to follow him. Once inside he took a seat at the table and waited for his visitor to do the same but he didn't bother with the recorder as he knew it would be a nonstarter and could possibly jeopardise the meeting if he tried to force the issue.

"I must say, I never expected to see one of Davey's men in a police station, well not voluntarily anyway, so how can I help?"

Gilly let of a loud weary sigh before he spoke and it was plain to see that he was troubled.

"I don't know if you can but you're my last hope. You remember Shauna?"

Neil Maddock frowned and for a second it felt as if someone had just walked over his grave, the feeling caused him to shudder.

"Of course I do, without her help we would never have nabbed your Boss, why, she's alright isn't she?"

"Firstly he isn't my Boss anymore, in fact I think it's safe to say that he's my arch-enemy. I helped Shauna get out of London and I've been out of the country myself for several months but I was called back after Shauna went missing. Now I have it on good authority that Davey has her but no one knows anything or at least if they do they

140

aren't saying. You know the score copper, people would rather die than speak ill or spread gossip about one of their own."

Now Neil Maddock was intrigued, if Wiseman had kidnapped the woman and they could prove it he would go down for years. Leaning forward in his seat Neil placed his elbows onto the table and clasped his hands in a prayer like pose.

"Tell me more, how do you know all of this?"

"Leave it out Copper, you really think I'm going to spill my fucking guts to the likes of you?"

Neil sighed heavily and then tapped his pursed lips with the index finger of his right hand.

"As strange as it might sound, yes I do. If I haven't got anything concrete to go on then how can I proceed?"

"Look Maddock! You owe her big style because if you'd have kept your fucking trap shut Wiseman would never have known it was her!"

"That might well be the case but without more information the door would be firmly shut regarding a fresh investigation."

Gilly thought for a moment and he began to regret ever coming here. The Old Bill couldn't be trusted everyone knew that and yet here he was confiding in one of the biggest bastards to ever work for The Met, or at least that was what Davey always said whenever the two men's paths had crossed.

"Look, the old girl who Shauna used to live with contacted me and told me she was missing. I came back and found out through a contact that Davey was holding her somewhere but he wouldn't say anything other than that. When I went back to quiz him again I found out he'd disappeared and I don't fucking have to expand on what that means now do I? So, are you going to help me or not?"

Neil Maddock once again began to tap on his bottom lip. The action was starting to get right up Gilly's nose and he tilted his head in such a way that it was obvious to the detective if he didn't answer soon the man was prepared to get up and walk out.

"Look, as much as it pains me to say it, you're going to have to leave this with me, I can't just snap my fingers and open a case. I need to take some advice, maybe even get permission if it's needed. Will you let me have your number?"

Neil slid an A4 pad and a pen across the table. Gilly looked the man directly in the eyes for several seconds trying to weigh up the situation to see if he was being set up. Convinced that all was good, he picked up the pen and quickly scribbled down the details of his mobile. Moments later and he was back out on the street. Breathing deeply he was sure his clothes now stank of the police but knew it was just his mind playing tricks. Heading for the Nell Gwynne Tavern on Bull Inn Court, Gilly knew he would be safe and away from prying eyes. The place was a little too upmarket to attract Davey's people and situated down a side alley it was also off of the beaten track. Ordering a pint of real ale Gilly took a seat in the corner and removed his mobile from his pocket. He didn't have a clue what he was hoping to accomplish by phoning the man but it had to at least be worth a try just in case Davey let something slip but Gilly very much doubted that would happen.

As usual Davey Wiseman was seated behind his desk at The Pelican, Jimbo and a couple of the others were out collecting the rent money, a euphemism for retracting protection money from a few of his regular clients. It was a racket Davey had been involved in for years but while he was banged up a couple of the regulars had decided that they no longer needed to pay. Jimbo had been sent to remind them that payment was long overdue and he'd been told in no uncertain terms not to return empty handed. When his mobile rang Davey glanced at the screen but didn't recognise the number.

"Yeah?"

"It's Gilly."

There was a short awkward silence for both of the men but it only lasted for a matter of seconds. Davey had accepted this call was on the horizon and he was fuming but hid it well. His tone was quite light as he spoke, well as light as it could be if your name was Davey Wiseman.

"I heard you were back and I must say you've got a fucking cheek. You do know this ain't going to end well and when I eventually catch up with you, well let's just say you will cease to exist in my eyes."

"So you're threatening me, now why doesn't that surprise me."

Davey was careful with his choice of words and after Gilly had shafted him once he wouldn't put anything past the man, even going to the police wasn't out of the question. There was good reason why Gilly would want to see him back inside and threatening to kill would be just what The Met would like to hear about.

"The thought never entered my head Gilly, you can be a right fucking drama queen when the mood takes you."

"We can trade insults and threats all day Davey but we both know that's not why I'm calling. I know you have her."

"Sorry son but I ain't got a fucking clue what you're on about, now if you'll excuse me I'm a very busy man. Unlike some who chose to rob from their employers, I have to earn my bread and butter."

Gilly thought back to when he'd let himself into Davey's apartment and had taken the hundred grand. It had never sat comfortably, that's why most of the money was still sitting in the luggage storage at Kings Cross station.

"I still have your cash and I'll get it back to you at some point. Now come on Davey, why don't you let her go?"

"Hypothetically, if I had her then there ain't a fucking cat in hells chance that you'll ever see her again but like I said I haven't. One last thing, I really fucking hope we meet up again soon Slade, it would really make my day!"

The line went dead and Gilly could see that his hand was shaking. The only option left was for Maddock to come through, if he didn't then Gilly knew he would never see Shauna again and that thought scared the hell out of him.

CHAPTER EIGHTEEN

Shauna was in the middle of changing JJ, the baby was lying on the hallway floor as she was in the habit of having a very messy nappy and Shauna didn't want to spoil the carpets. She knew it was ridiculous as this wasn't her home but her prison but she still had standards if nothing else. Hearing a car draw up outside she instantly froze. Slowly getting to her feet Shauna walked into the front room and peered out of the window. When she realised who it was her heart skipped a beat and she wanted to kick herself for feeling this way. Davey Wiseman, the father of her child but the man who was also holding her captive still had a hold over her and she wondered if these feelings, this longing, would ever disappear. As he walked through the door and met her gaze Davey couldn't take his eyes off of her. She was clean and dressed in the new clothes he had bought her and he didn't think she had ever looked more beautiful. They could have been the perfect family if it wasn't for the fact that he had to keep her here against her will but there was no way he would ever allow her to be free, it went against every code he'd followed since he first started out.

"So, you like the place?"

It was now Shauna's turn to study and no matter how hard she tried she couldn't hate him any longer, it wasn't now her life's work to make him suffer but if she could let go of the past then why couldn't he?

"Are you ever going to let us walk out of here?"

"Afraid not sweetheart, I told you how it was going to be and fuck me, ain't this good enough for you? There's nothing you need, I've provided everything and still

145

you're not fucking happy!"

"I need other people Davey, I need fresh air and to feel the grass under my feet."

"I don't think I'd ever have been able to please you but then again, you weren't with me out of love were you? This place cost a packet, I should have left you in that fucking basement but no, I only wanted the best for you."

JJ stirred and for a moment they both stopped talking as they waited for their daughter to begin crying but she just gurgled for a second and then fell asleep again.

"It's beautiful Davey and under normal circumstances I would have been so happy to live here, probably been happy for the rest of my life but it's not normal, we're prisoners. Surely to God you can see that you can't keep us locked up forever?"

"Can't I?"

"What if JJ gets ill, she's a child and bound to come down with things now and again and what about when it's time for her to start school?"

Davey walked from the hallway and into the front room as Shauna, clutching the baby to her chest, quickly followed after him.

"Well?"

"It's all sorted! You should know me better than that darlin', I never leave anything to chance, no, I take that back, the only time I did I paid the price by getting banged up and who's fault was that or has it conveniently slipped your fucking mind?"

Shauna didn't answer, she didn't know what to say.

"If my daughter gets sick I will have a doctor call at the house to treat her. When it's time for her education I will employ someone to do home schooling."

"Don't be so ridiculous! You don't honestly think you

146

can keep us here for years without anyone finding out do you?"

Davey began to laugh out loud and the sound instantly made Shauna angry. The raised voices woke JJ and she picked up on her mother's upset and began to cry but still Shauna wouldn't leave the matter.

"Well yes actually I do."

"You're insane!"

"Shauna, Shauna, Shauna, I have run my empire for almost forty years without anyone really knowing what I do, well at least I did until you came along. You think keeping you here will be difficult? It will be a piece of fucking cake sweetheart and never forget it!"

"But there's no need for all of this, you can trust me now honestly you can."

"Like I thought I could before you mean, like when you ripped out my fucking heart and then trampled all over it?"

"So this is what it all boils down to, punishment? So what about you Mr Wiseman, when will you be punished for beating my sister and me, for murdering my mum and Vonny, when exactly will you be made to pay?"

Here words cut like a knife, Davey had tried so hard to get those haunting images out of his mind and hearing the truth once again he couldn't handle it. Storming out of the house without another word he locked the front door, got into his Jag and tore off down the drive leaving Shauna sobbing as JJ screamed in fear.

The drive back to London was carried out in record time and Davey broke every speed limit on the road. He was so incensed, so full of rage at what she'd dare to say to him that he didn't give a thought to getting pulled over by

147

the Old Bill. Luck was on his side and when he at last came to a stop outside The Pelican he had finally calmed down. Passing the two doormen who in unison said 'Evening Mr Wiseman', Davey stepped into the place that always made him feel safe. The club was in full swing and Janice and the new barman were so busy that neither noticed him enter. Jimbo was patrolling the room as a warning to anyone that was thinking of being a bit naughty. A few blokes were getting slightly out of hand as they tried to attract the attention of a group of girls but soon quietened down when he walked over. All in all except for his one indiscretion at the Judge's Den, the man was shaping up well and Davey was now more than satisfied with Dickie Pinter's recommendation. About to head in the direction of his office, Davey was stopped when Max Scott approached him. Max had been a friend of Billy's from way back when they were all just starting out. He was a faggot but not the type who usually got under Davey's skin as he kept his sex life to himself and never promoted the fact that he was gay.

"Hello there Davey, long time no see, how you doing mate?"

"Hi Max, mustn't grumble but things could always be better. So what you doing round this neck of the woods, thought you was based over in Norwood Junction and everyone knows blokes from the Junction never leave their own manor?"

Max Scott laughed but Davey could see that it was false, that the man was here for a reason but was having difficulty broaching the subject.

"Fancy a chat in my office, you can't hear yourself think with all those leery cunts shouting and screaming."

Max smiled and nodded his head, it would be easier to be

148

the bearer of bad news when his voice could actually be heard and what he had to say didn't need to be shouted out for all and sundry to hear. Davey waited for Max to close the door then he walked over to the cabinet and poured them both a scotch. He didn't know why his visitor was here but it must be important and old Maxey really didn't look at ease.

"So, why have you stepped outside of the Junction and don't say for the club experience because this place is a shit hole, we both know it but it still brings in the reddies."

"I went to see The Baron today."

The Baron was a name Max had always used to refer to Billy Jackson and just the mention of it silenced Davey.

"I know you two ain't on good terms but he's sick Davey and I mean really fucking sick."

"Sick in the fucking head more like!"

"No I'm being serious here, really serious."

"What like cancer or something?"

Max shook his head and as his eyes filled with tears Davey suddenly felt scared. After the trial and ever since, he hadn't wanted anything to do with Billy, even felt as though he hated the man but hearing this news changed all that. Billy Jackson had been the bane of his life, had hated Shauna although thinking about it now he had been right on that score. The man had caused Davey immense amounts of aggravation over the years but when it came down to it, he had also been the best and most loyal friend anyone could wish for.

"Sadly, its Aids."

"The fucking gay plague, are you having a laugh Max?"

"I wish I was but no, Billy is terminal and coming to the end, it won't be more than a few months."

"How? No don't answer that, it was a silly fucking question. I only saw him a couple of weeks back and apart from being as mad as a box of fucking frogs, which as we both know isn't anything unusual where Billy is concerned. What I'm trying to say, is that he looked fine."

Max sighed heavily, he hated being the bearer of bad news and this was about as bad as it got.

"I know. No one knew but apparently he's had it for years but wouldn't tell the authorities so there was no medication. He'd been taking a cocktail of drugs for years and when he stopped, well the rot set in pretty quickly and now he's refusing any help. Seems the day you visited, well after you left actually, well he just went mental. Attacked one of the male nurses and took out both of the bloke's eyes. Don't get me wrong, I love old Billy you know I do but that was bang out of fucking order. They put him in solitary and he ain't been the same since, I think he's given up Davey. Even his own brothers won't visit in case they catch it, the thick cunts. Anyway, I've delivered what I came here to. Now it's up to you to decide if want to go and see him but if that's on your mind then I wouldn't leave it too long pal."

As he headed towards the door Max didn't say anything more and Davey just stood there feeling numb. He hadn't planned on ever setting foot in Broadmoor again but this was something different, if Billy died it would be the end of an era and a big part of Davey's life. He needed to think and to do that he needed to be alone, so slipping out of The Pelican without anyone inside even knowing he'd been there, Davey drove back to his apartment and the large bottle of scotch that he knew would be gone by the morning.

150

The night was long with memories invading his mind, some happy, some sad and a few that were downright hilarious and had him laughing out loud until the tears started to fall, tears for Billy, for their wasted lives but most of all tears for himself and all the hurt he had caused people for no other reason than he had to be in control, had to be in charge and show that no one got anything over on him.

After a restless night Davey was once again on the road. The traffic was light and by eleven that morning he was pulling into the vast car park of Broadmoor Hospital. After passing all the security checks he was shown into the medical centre where inmates who were physically sick were housed. Billy Jackson had been placed in a side room but the door was firmly locked as he was still seen as a danger to the staff and other patients. The first thing Davey noticed as he entered the room was a strange sickly smell that he could only liken to almonds or overripe pears. As he walked over to the bed he had to use all of his inner strength to hold back a gasp of shock that was desperately trying to escape. Billy was thin, pitifully thin and the reddish purple lesions on his cheek and neck looked terrible. Turning his head and seeing his visitor made Billy smile weakly.

"Why didn't you tell me Bill, all these fucking years and you never said a word, why?"

Billy's eyes were deeply sunken and his voice though audible, was very low in tone.

"Because it would have ruined our friendship Davey boy and that's something that meant the world to me. I knew if I shared my secret you'd distance yourself and I wouldn't have been able to handle that. I ain't got long

151

left."

"I know Max Scott called by The Pelican last night and thank fuck he did or I wouldn't have found out until......."
Davey couldn't bring himself to finish the sentence and as he wiped his eyes with the palm of his hand, the action warmed Billy's heart.

"You ain't going all fucking soft on me at this late stage in the day are you?"

The two men laughed and for just a short moment the years fell away to a time when they were young men just starting out, young men with plans to take over London and rule the city like Kings. The visit was short as Billy tired easily and when it was time to leave Davey bent over the bed and kissed his old friend on the forehead. No goodbyes were said, none were needed but they both knew this would be the last time they would ever see each other, on this mortal coil at least.

CHAPTER NINETEEN

Gilly had been lurking about unseen outside The Pelican for a couple of days now, he'd then moved on to Davey's apartment but it didn't take him long to realise that without a car it was futile and a complete waste of his time. He was able to monitor the man and some strange bloke, or Man Mountain Benny as he had nick named Jimbo, coming and going but every time Davey went out anywhere Gilly wasn't able to follow him so what was the point? There was only one thing for it and it really went against the grain as he would feel like a common thief but there was nothing left to do, so taking the bull by the horns Gilly made his way over to Kings Cross station and retrieved the holdall containing Davey's money. Taking it back to Linda's flat on Rowley Way he was as nervous as hell as he walked along the narrow lanes that separated the blocks of flats. Mugging was common place on the estate and there were plenty of unsavoury characters milling around here but then no one except him knew what was inside the bag and in all honesty, Gilly Slade didn't look like he had two penny's to rub together so no one was interested in rolling him over. Opening the front door he called out but luckily his sister-in-law had gone down the market, so retreating to his room he placed a chair under the door handle in case she returned unexpectedly. Unzipping the bag Gilly pushed the money as far as he could to one side and began to rummage along the bottom. He was sure the key fob to Davey's apartment was still inside and when his hand skimmed over the smooth piece of plastic he sighed with relief. It was going to be dangerous as Davey Wiseman didn't have a schedule and he could return at any given moment but as Maddock hadn't got back to him he had nowhere left to turn. Gilly decided that he would get up early the next day and wait for his old boss to go out, he knew the apartments layout and if luck was on his side and he found any clues, he could be in and out in a matter of minutes. After securing the holdall with a padlock Gilly stuffed it under the bed and by the amount of dust he found he didn't think Linda would find it. He giggled to himself when he thought of how house proud his sister-in-law always seemed, top show, that's what his old mum would have said.

By eight thirty the next morning he had positioned himself in a shop doorway across the road from the Mayfair apartment block. Davey's was the top floor penthouse but there was no movement from inside or none that Gilly could see. At nine on the dot the Jag pulled up outside and Gilly eyed the driver as it was the first time he'd been able to study the man for any length of time. It was now obvious he was Gilly's replacement and when Davey emerged and the driver got out to open the back door, Gilly couldn't believe the size of the man. James Hardy might have looked like an Adonis but he was also built like a brick shit house and Gilly was glad that they wouldn't be coming face to face with each other or at least he hoped they wouldn't. After the Jag pulled away he waited a couple of minutes and then crossed the road.

Nervously entering the main foyer Gilly's eyes were instantly drawn to the close circuit television. On his last visit here which was months earlier, he hadn't noticed them but then again he hadn't been looking and that was a different scenario entirely. Stopping for a moment he thought long and hard and as long as he didn't act suspiciously there was no reason why his entry should be reported to Davey, if it was? Well, it wouldn't really make any difference apart from the fact that he would wind the man up even more than he already had done. Taking the elevator up to the top floor he swiped the fob which enabled him to open the lift door and walk straight into the apartment. Nothing had changed apart from the fact that the last visit had been taken at a slow place, this time he had to act fast. Starting in the bedroom, he wasn't there more than a few minutes as the contemporary furniture was minimal and after opening the bedside drawers he found nothing. The front room was the same although the space was so vast it would take slightly longer and only half way through his search Gilly was about to open up a small cupboard that was beside one of the sofas when he heard a low murmuring sound. Running over to the door he pressed his ear to the surface, it was definitely coming from the lift shaft. It could be someone from the lower floors but when the sound became louder he panicked as he looked around for somewhere to hide. The kitchen was as good a place as any and entering his eyes darted for a space to conceal himself, the only option was a floor to ceiling cabinet that housed a vacuum cleaner and squeezing himself inside he slowly closed the door.

Davey had forgotten his wallet which wouldn't have normally bothered him as he would have raided the petty cash from one of the clubs but today he was buying a gift for his little girl and it had to be above board so he needed his credit card. Stepping out of the lift he had a funny sensation that he wasn't alone but glancing around there was nothing untoward and he chastised himself for being stupid. Gilly heard the front door open and was aware that he was breathing heavily and prayed that he wouldn't cough or sneeze involuntarily. Gilly heard someone enter the kitchen and he clasped his open palm over his mouth and nose in an attempt to quieten his breathing which in all honesty was no different than usual but to him it sounded rapid and loud.

Spying the black Gucci wallet on the work surface Davey grabbed it and was about to push it into his pocket when he had the strange feeling again. Stopping dead in his tracks he listened intently for any sound and then laughed as he spoke out loud.

"Wiseman you're losing the fucking plot mate."

It wasn't until he heard the front door close that Gilly removed his hand and allowed himself to take in a deep lungful of air. It had been a close call and he knew that if Davey had found him, then he would never have left the flat again, well at least not while he was still breathing. Stepping from the cupboard Gilly walked into the front room and gingerly crept over to the gigantic window that spanned across the entire width of the room and peered down to make absolutely sure that Davey had gone. When he saw the man climb into the Jag and the car speed off he at last breathed a sigh of relief. His shirt was sticking to the skin on his back where he'd perspired so heavily in fear and he was desperate to take a shower. Glancing around the room there wasn't much left to hold his interest and with the study now the only place left to look he walked along the hallway with a heavy heart. The first thing he saw as he entered was a massive desk and the two or three piles of papers that sat on top. After scanning and then rejecting them as unimportant he moved them to one side. Opening up the drawers' one at a time he began to methodically search through each but there was nothing that gave him any clues. Closing the last one he then started to reposition the papers on top when something caught his eye. What was Davey doing with a letter from an estate agency? There were no details of a property it only congratulated him on his purchase. Something intrigued Gilly, why would Davey Wiseman be buying a property from a firm out in Welwyn Garden City? There was absolutely nothing to suggest that it had anything to do with Shauna but Gilly still had a gut feeling that he couldn't ignore. Removing his phone he tapped the address into his contact folder and then slipped out of the apartment.

When he was at last back in Linda's flat he laid down on the bed and thought of what to do next. He couldn't just rock up at the agents and start to ask questions as he knew he would be met with a wall of silence, client confidentiality and all that bollocks, no Gilly had to have a reason to call there. Suddenly it came to him, he would make an appointment to view a house and without pondering on the idea too long he picked up his mobile and rang the agents.

"Good afternoon Garden Estate Agency, how may I direct your call?"

The woman spoke with a plum in her mouth and Gilly knew that it must be one of those upmarket places that always seemed to overvalue anything they were selling. With the best and most articulate accent he could manage he began to speak. It didn't sound too bad apart from the odd word that came out all East End but all in all he was pleased with his act.

"Oh hello, I'm interested in purchasing a house and you

did such a sterling job for a mate of mine that he has highly recommended you."

Gilly realised when he'd first set his plan in motion that he was taking a risk but after weighing up the pro's and con's had come to the conclusion that there was no real reason why the company would contact Davey and start to ask questions.

"Well of course Sir, might I ask who your friend is?"

"Mr Wiseman, Davey Wiseman."

"Oh yes, a lovely gentleman, would you just excuse me for a second?"

Gena Musgrave the receptionist waved in the direction of Gavin Withers and then placed Gilly on hold while she quickly explained who was on the phone. All who worked at Garden Estates were still revelling in the accolade they had received from the partners in securing such a large sale and completing so swiftly. Now it appeared that there might be the chance of a repeat performance and in the same calendar month as well.

"Good morning, Gavin Withers speaking now I understand you are looking to purchase a property Sir?"

"Yes that's correct. I don't really mind where it is but it has to be bigger and more expensive than Mr Wiseman's, we have a bit of friendly rivalry going on. I forgot to mention, it must be vacant so that I can proceed quickly as I'm only in the country for a few days."

Gavin clenched his fist and punched the air in a euphoric motion. If he could pull another big sale off he would get employee of the month, not to mention a very nice bonus on top. Gilly knew that by asking to view a vacant property he would have all the time he need to be alone with the man though he really hoped it wasn't going to take too long.

"Well you've come to the right place Mr?"

"Soames, Reginald Soames."

Gilly face grimaced in embarrassment, where the fuck had he plucked that one from? He'd been put on the spot and now wanted to laugh as it was the first name that had entered his head. He didn't want to use his own name but Reginald Soames? Really?

"Well if you would care to pop into the office tomorrow morning Mr Saomes I would be happy to show you what we currently have available, maybe even view a few properties if you have the time?"

"That sounds splendid Gavin, oh and Gavin?"

"Yes Mr Soames?"

"Can we keep this between ourselves for the moment, only I don't want Davey getting wind that I'm trying to outsize or outspend him."

Gilly made an attempt at laughter and was joined by the agent and both were being false but for different reasons entirely.

"Mum's the word Mr Soames, mum's the word. I look forward to meeting you tomorrow."

Gilly ended the call with a broad grin on his face suddenly this detective work was becoming very interesting. He didn't sleep well that night, he was anxious about the meeting but also excited as this was the first positive lead he'd had since he'd began but Gilly also knew he had to make sure that he didn't balls it all up by saying something too stupid early on. In the dark of the night he made plans of how he was going to carry out the visit. By the next morning he was in a highly agitated state and Linda could only watch in amusement as he busied himself in the kitchen but not really doing anything.

"You okay Gilly?"

"Yeah, why do you ask?"

"Because sweetheart, you've put three teabags in your cup! Now you're either on a promise or up to something?"

"Don't be bloody daft, I'm just in a good mood. Linda Slade you can be a right fucking suspicious cow at times."

Linda laughed and at the same time she tried to read her brother-in-law's expression.

"I was married to your brother remember and he was a right crafty sod when the mood took him."

Gilly laughed but didn't offer his sister-in-law any information which slightly pissed her off. The station near South Hampstead went directly to Welwyn so he didn't have to walk too far and when he was finally seated on the train and heading out of London he could at last sit back and relax, everything was in place, well it was mentally at least.

CHAPTER TWENTY

Arriving at Welwyn station Gilly made his way out of the Howard Centre shopping mall but didn't have a clue where he had to go. Stopping an elderly lady who was pushing a trolley and who seemed to be on a mission, he asked directions to Parkway. The woman looked at him as if he was incredibly stupid and with a stabbing motion of her finger, pointed to the end of the walkway and then stormed off without a word being spoken. Gilly smiled, sighed at the woman's ignorance and continued on his way. As he reached the corner he instantly saw his destination and was glad at least that he hadn't had to do a marathon to get there. His mismatched jacket and trousers appeared somewhat eccentric but he had managed to find an old briefcase and a tie which was still hanging in Linda's wardrobe, he imagined it was a relic from the days when his brother had lived there though why she had held onto it he hadn't got a clue. Pushing on the door his acting came to the fore, he had to appear wealthy if a little mad. Gilly hoped his appearance would help with this but in all honesty it had been the best he could muster at such short notice. The first to greet him was Gena Musgrave and she gave him a strange look as she smiled.

"Good morning Sir, how may I help?"

In his most up market accent Gilly explained that he was here to see a Gavin Withers and Gena was out of her chair in a second and showing him over to one of the plush sofas while at the same time offering tea, coffee or even a soft drink. Gilly declined them all and looked at his watch signalling that he was tight for time. The look didn't go unnoticed and with a smile Gena disappeared

161

into one of the rear offices, seconds later Gavin Withers came bounding through with a folder in one hand and the other eagerly extended before he'd even got anywhere near Gilly.

"Mr Soames I'm so pleased to meet you."

"Likewise I'm sure."

Gavin took a seat on the sofa beside him which was a bit too close for comfort as far as Gilly was concerned. As he spoke Gavin studied the man, his clothes were odd and mismatched but then the city types could be off the wall at times and if Mr Soames knew Mr Wiseman he must have money to burn so as far as Gavin was concerned he didn't care if his client was start bullock naked as long as he intended to spend a vast amount of cash.

"Now I've taken the liberty of choosing three properties that we currently have on our books and all I might add are considerably larger and more expensive than the one your friend Mr Wiseman's purchased."

They both laughed as the estate agent handed over the folder and Gilly feigned interest as he flicked through it. It was a complete waste of his time as he knew that the first property they visited would allow him enough time alone with the man to find out all he needed to know.

"Where did you park Mr Soames?"

"I didn't as I came on the train, actually I find it so tedious trying to drive in the city and as I'm out of the country so much of the time there really isn't any point in having a vehicle. Shall we go?"

Gavin was on his feet in seconds and he was so desperate to seal a deal that he almost headed out of the door without his client. The men drove about four miles out of Welwyn before pulling into a very grand driveway. Gavin waited for a response of wow or isn't it fabulous

162

but there was nothing and he assumed that the lack of a reaction to the property and all of its grandeur was probably due to the fact that it was nothing out of the ordinary for his client. What he didn't realise was that Gilly was actually thinking that the mock Georgian house was vast and he wondered at how the other half lived.

"This property is vacant isn't it?"

"Of course Mr Soames, I followed your instructions to the letter, shall we?"

Gavin unlocked the front door and allowed Gilly to enter the enormous hallway first. As far as Gavin was concerned if this didn't sell the place nothing would and as he stepped inside and closed the heavy front door he had a broad grin on his face.

"Wonderful isn't it?"

Gilly didn't reply and as he walked into one of the rooms leading from the hall way he started to talk.

"So where exactly is the house Davey bought?"

Suddenly Gavin was on his guard. Surely if the men were close friends then Mr Wiseman would have shared the address.

"I'm sorry but I can't give out that information, client confidentiality and all that. Now these storage units are bespoke and made out of the finest walnut and....."

Gavin was about to continue his sales pitch but was stopped when he came face to face with a large knife that Gilly had removed from his briefcase. Mr Soames had disappeared and in his place was someone from the East End, someone who wasn't about to leave until he had some answers or until blood had been spilt trying to get those answers.

"What are you doing, oh my God you're insane!"

"Right you smarmy little cunt! I'm going to ask you

163

some questions and if I was you I would answer very fucking quickly or you and this little beauty are going to get very well acquainted."

The sound and smell of urine running onto the highly polished marble floor made then both look downwards and when Gavin burst into tears and began to blubber like a baby Gilly was taken aback but not enough for it to soften his assault. Taking a step forward he poked the young man in the chest with the tip of the knife and it was enough for Gavin to metaphorically spill his guts.

"Whoever you are I will tell you anything you want to know but please, please don't hurt me, pleeeeease!"

"Where is the house Davey Wiseman bought?"

"It's in Burnham Green, just up the road from here, a house called Journeys End Defiant. Mr Wiseman was insistent that he completed the sale in a matter of days and wasn't worried about any of the legal stuff. Please can I go now, the office will be wondering where I am."

"No they won't you lying cunt we're supposed to go to two more houses remember?"

"Is that what you want to do?"

Davey couldn't believe how thick the bloke was and slowly shook his head as he spoke. His eyes appeared to have narrowed and to Gavin he looked very menacing.

"No it isn't now take me to the house you just told me about."

"But I can't it's.................."

Gavin didn't get to finish his sentence as Gilly sliced the knife down his cheek. In a split second the front door was yanked open and the agent was running towards his car. The wound was little more than a paper cut but by the way the man was acting anyone would have thought he'd been stabbed. Gilly followed in hot pursuit in case he had any ideas of speeding off and going to the Old Bill.

"Not so fast you little wanker, now do as I say and you won't get hurt."

"But you've just stabbed me!"

The man was vastly overstating the wound but Gilly was actually shocked at the amount of blood being shed.

"I ain't fucking stabbed anyone you fucking pussy! Now drive and take me to Davey's house."

Gavin did exactly as he'd been told and within a matter of minutes they pulled up in front of a large set of gates that were locked to keep prying eyes at bay. As he got out of the car Gilly turned to the driver and wore his most menacing expression.

"Now, I hope you ain't got any ideas about running to the filth because if you do, I will come back and slice you up good and fucking proper. You will not get in contact with Mr Wiseman nor will you mention to another living soul what has occurred today. Do I make myself fucking clear?"

Gavin Withers vigorously nodded his head and Gilly had a feeling he would keep his word, after all, the little tosser wouldn't want to have to explain to everyone why he pissed himself and cried like a baby. It had been plain to see when Gilly had first stepped foot inside the Estate Agents that Gavin saw himself as the office stud and admitting to what had happened to him would do his credibility no good whatsoever. Slamming the door Gilly waited until the car had disappeared down the road and then turned to study the gates, house name and general lie of the land. A six foot high wall surrounded the property and walking on a bit so that he was away from the main entrance he scaled the wall. As Gilly walked through the wooded grounds he had to give it to Davey, the man had taste.

When the house came into view he stopped for a second and surveyed it. There were no vehicles in front but what struck him the most were the iron grills on all of the windows. It didn't take a genius to work out that they had been installed to keep people out or was it to keep someone in, he prayed it was the latter. Slowly approaching Gilly felt like a Ninja as he darted in and out making his way around the property. Every so often he would bob his head up and look through a window but there was no sign of life until he went to the rear and what he imagined was the kitchen window. Seated at the table and as beautiful as ever was the love of his life. Shauna had just given JJ her bottle and was gently humming trying to get the baby off to sleep. Gilly lightly tapped on the window as he didn't want to scare her. As Shauna looked up she strained her eyes though the gaps in the intricate metal work trying to make out who was there. Suddenly she realised who it was and Gilly could see her mouth the words 'Oh my God!' as the palm of her hand flew up to her mouth. He beckoned for her to come over but she pointed towards the next room before disappearing. Gilly was apprehensive, was she trying to tell him that there was someone in the house with her? But then again she didn't seem like she was panicking. Slowly he moved along the outer wall and saw that behind the railing she had opened the window an inch. "Oh Gilly!!! It's so good to see you, I've prayed and prayed that one day I would see you again. This is the only window in the house that will open because of these."

Shauna pointed to the bespoke ironwork with tears

streaming down her face. In his nervous state Gilly was about to come out with something inane and meaningless but as quick as a flash she disappeared. When she re-emerged a moment later he understood where she'd gone to and now the tears had been wiped away and Shauna wore the most beautiful smile as she held the bundle up to the window.

"Meet JJ."

"Oh my God Shauna she's gorgeous, looks just like her mum."

"How did you find me Gilly? I thought we were going to be locked away here forever."

The tears started again and his heart was aching to take her in his arms and tell her everything was going to be fine but he couldn't and anyway, he wasn't sure that things would be fine.

"It's a long story sweetheart but now that I know where you are I'm going to do my damnedest to get you out. It might take me a while but you know I won't let you down."

"You mean you can't get me out today? Oh no Gilly please help us, I can't stand much more of this."

Reaching into his pocket to retrieve his phone he couldn't believe that it wasn't there. It had probably fallen out in the car of that knob Gavin or in the woods somewhere but either way he couldn't summon any help.

"Look babe I ain't got a phone with me and there's nothing here that will get these bastards off."

Gilly slammed his palm onto The Metalwork in frustration, her eyes looked so sad and so lonely and seeing her in that state made the anger inside Gilly Slade rise to heights that he had never experienced.

"I'm going to get off now sweetheart but I promise you

167

from the bottom of my heart that I will be back, in the next couple of days I will be back to get you out."
Gilly squeezed his hand sideways through the railings and with a painful struggle managed to lift just the tips under the opened window. From her side Shauna did the same and when their fingers touched they both smiled.
"I know you will Gilly, you've never let me down before. I need you to know something, I was coming to the airport that day, honestly I was, only Davey's men got to me first."
Those few words were like music to his ears, words he never imagined that he would hear. Blowing her a kiss he ran off in the direction of the woods and Shauna closed the window, still crying but with a massive smile on her face.

CHAPTER TWENTY ONE

Two days after Gilly Slade's visit to the police station Neil Maddock had finally been able to get an appointment with Chief Inspector Graham Myers. It wasn't that his old friend wouldn't see him but purely down to the fact that the man had been out of the country for a few days. Entering the building of New Scotland Yard, Neil went through the rigorous security checks and then made his way up to the Inspector's office. As usual he was greeted with a friendly hand shake and the Inspector relaxed thing when he said that no formalities were necessary.

"So Neil what can I do for you?"

Neil took a seat, grimaced and at the same time scratched his temple, he already had a gut feeling what the answer would be but he had to at least try.

"I know you won't like what I'm about to ask Graham but will you just let me finish before you reply?"

Graham nodded but his forehead wore a frown and like the man sitting in front of him, he had a good idea of what this entailed and what his response would be.

"Now I know you told me to walk away from Davey Wiseman and honestly I had until a few days ago. Out of the blue one of his former employees paid me a visit at the station and if you know these men, then you'll also know that his action was no mean feat in itself. Anyway, he told me that the woman involved in the case, Shauna O'Malley, has been abducted and he knows that it's Davey who is holding her against her will."

"And has she been reported as missing?"

"Well no but...."

"Neil, neither I nor you and most certainly not Davey

169

Wiseman, are above the law but this is a very tenuous accusation. The man has recently been released on appeal and the press would have a fucking field day with this if we go in all guns blazing and it doesn't result in an arrest. I can picture it now, not to mention the fact that Wiseman would probably sue The Met for an entire month's budget."

"So we just forget about the woman after she helped us put a villain behind bars?"

"Don't you mean a villain that was back out on the street and I might add, in less than six months! I'm sorry Neil but unless you can bring me concrete evidence and I mean fucking concrete, then my answer is no. We are friends and because of that I am going to do something that really goes against the grain. On this occasion I actually have to pull rank and order you to walk away or face serious consequences, do you understand me?"

"Yes Sir."

The informal conversation that had begun when Detective Maddock had entered the room was now well and truly over and in its place a resentment that he had never felt towards his superior before. Saying goodbye Neil left The Yard and made his way back to Agar Street and the case he was involved in but one which held little appeal and was in fact boring him to tears.

Gilly Slade, after hitching a lift into Welwyn had caught a train back to London but he hadn't returned to his sister-in-law's flat. Telling Shauna that it might be a couple of days turned out not to be an option, after seeing her he wouldn't rest until she was free and standing beside him. The train he caught didn't go to South Hampstead, instead he exited at Kings Cross Station and walked along Pentonville Road until he came to Gabby Jacob's hardware store. It was a miracle that the small shop was still trading after decades in the same location but the fact that most of North London's villains used it to tool up for jobs and Gabby knowing when to keep his trap shut, were probably the biggest factors in its survival. He selected wisely and after purchasing a crowbar and hammer Gilly went straight back to the station and boarded his second train out of the capital. His nerves were all over the place and he made sure not to make eye contact with anyone as the last thing he needed was for someone to strike up a conversation. For the second time that day he walked out of Welwyn Station and following the same route as before made his way through the Howard Centre. The bus station was situated to his right and stopping the first driver he could find, enquired as to when the next bus would be leaving for Burnham Green.

"Not your day sunshine, it's just left."

It wasn't what Gilly had hoped to hear and he was even more pissed off when told that it would be another forty minutes until the next one. Hanging around the shopping centre to kill some time he prayed that he wouldn't come face to face with Gavin or any of the man's colleagues. Luck was on his side and when the bus finally pulled into the depot Gilly was the first person to get on board. It had been a swift journey when he'd been in the car with the estate agent but not this time, this time it felt like an eternity due to the fact that there seemed to be someone waiting to get on at every single stop. When Gilly finally got off and stepped onto the lane he took a seat on a fallen tree trunk at the side of the road to take stock of the situation, so much had happened and now that it was almost over he didn't quite know how to proceed. Nothing was ever cut and dried and he just hoped that the tools he'd purchased would be man enough for the job. It was only a short walk to reach the gates that separated him from the only woman he had ever truly loved but it might as well have been miles, his nerves were so bad, his stomach was in knots and his lips were so dry that it felt as if his tongue was sticking to the roof of his mouth. Opposite the entrance to 'Journey's End Defiant' Gilly spied a telephone box. It was one of the old style red ones that you hardly saw anymore or if you did they were used to house a defibrillator or as a novelty library but having lost his mobile he had little choice than to give it a try. Pulling open the door he was doubtful that it would be working but crossed his fingers in hope anyway. Once again luck was on his side and tapping in the number for directory inquiries he asked for Agar Street Police Station and then to be put through. By the time his call was answered he had already fed in one pound fifty and at this rate he would be out of change before he'd got to speak to the one person that mattered. Neil Maddock had only just returned when he was told that someone wished to talk to him and when informed as to whom it was he sighed heavily.

He wasn't looking forward to relaying all that Graham Myers had said.

"Hi Gilly, it's not looking good I'm ...."

Gilly wasn't interested in what the man had to say, it was far too late for that. All he wanted was to pass on the address and explain what he was about to do, just in case anything should go wrong.

"You're where! What the hell do you think you're doing?"

"Well none of you cunts are prepared to help her so it's up to me ain't it?"

Neil knew this could all very quickly turn bad but he was also aware that it might be his last chance to collar Wiseman. With total disregard for the order he'd received to leave things alone, he commandeered two of his detectives, several uniformed officers along with a fleet of squad cars. No one was privy to the operation and if he failed his career could be on the line but for once Neil Maddock didn't care. He knew that if he broke all of the rules and switched on the blues and twos they could be out of London and at the address pretty fast, or at least by City standards.

Gilly climbed the wall and then started to walk through the woods towards the house. His hands were shaking but nothing was going to stop him getting Shauna and the baby out. As before, he walked around to the back of the house and tapped on the kitchen window but she was nowhere to be seen. Gilly frowned, had something happened, no it couldn't have in such a short space of time surely. Moving along he then tapped on the front room window and in seconds she was staring straight back at him. Tears streamed down her face and as Gilly held up the crowbar and hammer and then pointed in the direction of the front door Shauna silently mouthed the words 'thank you' over and over again.

Gilly placed the flat end of the crowbar between the door and the frame and holding the hammer, hit it several times with as much force as he could muster. Apart from a vast amount of noise nothing much happened. The ornate oak door showed a few chips and scratches but no substantial damage. He wasn't giving up that easy. Shauna shouted that there were also dead locks situated at

173

the top and bottom and Gilly knew from past experience that it would probably be impossible for him to break in. Moving to the rear door his heart sunk when he saw that it was identical to the front. Inside Shaun listened intently for any sign that her dear friend was winning but there was nothing.

Davey had been yearning to see the two women who were now the most important people in his life and leaving his apartment he instructed his minder to take him over to the house. Arriving at the property, Jimbo got out, unlocked the gates and then moved the car forward. He knew without being told that the grounds had to remain secure at all times, so he then closed the gates and locked them before continuing along the driveway.

Gilly was frustrated at his failure to gain entry and returning to the front of the property, like a man possessed he violently attacked the door once more but didn't hear a car approach until it screeched to a halt. The doors flew open and Jimbo and Davey raced over. Within seconds Jimbo had Gilly by the throat and Davey opened up the door as quickly as he could. JJ who was lying on the hall floor, a place Shauna had found that the little girl liked, began to scream at the top of her lungs. As soon as the front door opened Shauna ducked under her kidnappers arm and ran outside quickly followed by Davey. Anger engulfed her and she flew into a rage and jumped onto Jimbo's back. Clawing at the man's eyes made him loosen his grip on Gilly and turning he punched her fully in the face. Shauna fell to the floor as Gilly grabbed the crowbar. Lashing out in Jimbo's direction he hit the man squarely across the back. Jimbo turned, his face full of pain and rage and as he dived in

Gilly's direction, Davey grabbed Shauna's arm and pulled
her to safety. She resisted him and tried to shake his
hand from her wrist but it only made him grip tighter.
Jimbo was getting stuck into Gilly and in response Gilly
was fighting back with every ounce of strength he could
conjure up. Davey was amazed, he hadn't realised his
ex-employee could take care of himself so well, true
when it came down to size he was no match for Jimbo but
he was still giving it a cracking good go. Suddenly the
two men fell through the open front door as they wrestled
like maniacs for control and dominance. With Davey in
tow Shauna ran forward but stopped dead in her tracks
when she heard a single muffled cry and then silence. A
second later she could hear sobbing and moving forward
she began to slowly shake her head. Davey then passed
her and ran inside, the sight that greeted him made him
drop to his knees. In their desperate attempt to beat each
other to a pulp, the two men had stumbled into the
hallway but hadn't seen JJ. Jimbo had punched Gilly in
the stomach with full force and doubled over in agony,
Gilly had fallen to the floor. Tragically he hadn't missed
the baby and like a dead weight he landed right on top of
her. JJ's tiny limp body was motionless and Davey
instinctively knew that she was dead. Fear engulfed him
as he turned and saw Shauna step inside. Her movements
were so rigid and wooden that they resembled an action
being played out in slow motion but then it stopped when
she let out the most piercing heart-breaking scream.
"No! No! No! What have you done, in God's name
what have you done. My baby, my poor, poor
baby!!!!!!!"
Shauna was instantly down on the floor and grabbing JJ's
lifeless body, held her to her chest, almost as if holding

her close she would somehow be able to bring her back to life. Davey reached out to touch her but one look from Shauna's cold hard eyes made him retract his hand. Kissing the top of JJ's head she again began to scream but this time there was no build up to her tears, this time they came thick and fast as if her very heart had been ripped out. Neil Maddock's car pulled up outside the gates just as Shauna screamed and the haunting noise was one he knew he would never forget. Ordering a detective to fetch the enforcer, the nickname given to the steel battering ram that they carried in the boot of the car, the gates were opened swiftly and with little effort. The cars soon roared up the driveway and screeching to a halt the area was immediately swarming with uniformed officers. As Neil ran into the house the scene that greeted him was horrendous and when he looked in Gilly Slade's direction, the man could only hang his head as tears streamed down his cheeks. Running over, Neil tried to take the baby from Shauna in a vain attempt to resuscitate the child but Shauna only held on tighter and no amount of gentle pleading could convince her to hand over the baby. As she sobbed uncontrollably Neil got to his feet and ordered an ambulance, though in all honesty he knew there was little point. Tapping Davey on the shoulder he motioned for him to step outside. When they were away from prying ears Neil and Davey had the first albeit brief, proper two way conversation to ever pass between them.
"What the hell has just happened here?"
"It was just a stupid fucking fight that resulted in a tragic accident copper, though what the fuck you're doing here I ain't got a clue. Now if you don't mind, my daughter has just died so I'd like some privacy and for you and your fucking Muppets to get out of my house and off of my

land."

"I bet you would but it ain't going to happen pal. A child has died in suspicious circumstances and for all I know it could have been you that killed her."

Davey had never felt rage for another human being like he did right now and grabbing the collar of Detective Maddock's jacket he was about to land a head butt when his arms were grabbed by two uniformed officers and he was pushed to the ground.

"Cuff this cunt, stick him in the car and then round up the others. Not the woman though, I'll bring her in myself once the ambulance has arrived."

Davey began to resist but it was futile.

"On what fucking charge copper?"

Neil smiled in a mocking manner, this really was turning out to be a good day.

"Probably the worst one possible, murdering a child!"

"You cunt!!!!! I'm going to take great fucking pleasure in ending your career Maddock and by the time I've finished The Met won't have a budget big enough to run a single station!"

"Sure you are Davey, sure you are and now I'm shaking in my fucking boots."

When the car door slammed shut Neil walked towards the house and his mind was racing. He'd broken all the rules and when the shit did hit the fan he would probably be out on his ear but no matter how much trouble he was in, he couldn't worry about that now. Now he had to wind things up here and then make sure that the poor little cow inside was taken care of.

CHAPTER TWENTY TWO

Back at Agar Street police station things didn't go to plan as far as Neil Maddock was concerned. There was no way he could charge Davey Wiseman as there were too many others involved and as yet the circumstances regarding the crime, if indeed there had actually been a crime, were unclear. The only option left open to the detective was to interview each person in turn but he had no evidence to hold anyone after the interviews were concluded and Davey would only reiterate what he had stated earlier, that it was a tragic accident. Gilly Slade, pissed off at the lack of help offered when he had asked a few days before wasn't keen to cooperate and James Hardy, AKA Jimbo, took a leaf from his army training and refused to utter a single word. Neil's only hope was Shauna but the woman was so traumatised and in shock that she just stared blankly into space as if her very soul had been torn out and there was absolutely nothing left inside.

Deciding that he would do more harm than good, at least as far as his career was concerned if he detained anyone further, at least not until an autopsy had taken place and any possible evidence had come to light, he reluctantly released them all, though not at the same time. Neil had an inkling that two of the people wouldn't want to be within a mile of Davey Wiseman so Shauna O'Malley and Gilly Slade were allowed to leave first and as Neil watched the man gently guide her down the steps and out into the rear courtyard his heart went out to them. He could see that Gilly adored this woman, a woman he knew that after the events of a few hours ago, would never be the same again. A squad car had been instructed

to take them to the address Gilly had given on Rowley
Way but not before Detective Maddock had warned them
that they must be available for further interviews at a later
date. Jimbo was next but he didn't go far and waited
outside in the hope that his boss would soon follow but
when Davey finally emerged he wasn't interested in
conversation. Hailing a cab the only words he uttered to
his employee were 'Go and fetch the car' before he
jumped into the taxi and it sped off down the road.

Slowly getting out of the police car, Shauna took in
nothing of her surroundings. Her mind was blank and
she couldn't yet grieve the loss of JJ but what hurt even
more was the fact that she couldn't picture her baby, not a
single image no matter how hard she tried would come to
mind. Gilly tenderly held her elbow as they made their
way down one of the many walkways. People passed by,
all busily unaware of the atrocity that had just occurred
and like any other day there were no good mornings or
cheery smiles on offer. London could and was on most
occasions, the loneliest place on earth if you happened to
be in a bad mind set. Opening up the front door Gilly
gently ushered Shauna inside and then led her straight to
his room. Inviting her to take a seat on the bed he then
went to find Linda. Gilly had secretly hoped that she
would be out, hoped for just a short while to gather his
thoughts but when he heard the radio playing in the
kitchen, knew that wasn't to be. As he stood leaning up
against the doorframe he stared in Linda's direction but
didn't say a word. Reading a magazine while Aretha
Franklins' 'Respect' blared out from the radio Linda
didn't even look up as she spoke.
"I was starting to get a bit worried about you, one day

you're sat in front of that bloody box for twenty four hours and the next you just disappear."

Glancing up she stopped her line of conversation when she noticed the serious expression on her brother-in-law's face."

"What's up you look as white as a sheet?"

"I've got a favour to ask. My friend needs a bed for a few nights and ......"

"Oh no you don't Gilly Slade! What do you think I'm running here a fucking B & B or something?"

"Please Linda, just hear me out. I got in a spot of bother fighting and well a baby accidently died and......"

"What the fuck!"

"It isn't as bad as it sounds, what the fuck am I saying? Of course it's as bad as it sounds, worse even but what I mean is, it was a freak accident and we have to stay local as the Old Bill want to interview us in the next few days and Shauna, God love her, ain't got no place else to go."

"And just who the fuck is Shauna?"

"She's the mother of the little girl who died and a very special friend to me. Please Linda, help the poor little cow out."

Gilly had always been a bit of a lad and Linda knew that no woman had ever touched his heart, well they hadn't until now. The look of sadness on his face said it all though, it was a mixture of sadness and happiness combined. Linda instantly changed her attitude, never having children of her own, though that was a case of circumstances rather than choice, she now felt a deep sense of loss for the woman.

"Of course she can stay but you'll have to take the sofa. Why don't you go and fetch her and I'll make some fresh tea?"

Gilly nodded his thanks and went through to the bedroom but Shauna had lain down and was now asleep or at least he thought she was, she might have been feigning it so that he would leave her alone and who could blame her if she was. Gently closing the bedroom door he returned to the kitchen to explain all that had happened in the hope that his sister-in-law might be able to offer some consolation although he very much doubted it, not when she heard who else was involved.

Davey had returned to his apartment and the feeling of loss that invaded his mind was all consuming. Storming from room to room the frustration built up until he lashed out and punched the highly polished study door. To say his action left a mark was an understatement, the door was beyond repair. Davey wanted, no he needed, to be with Shauna but he didn't have a clue where she was. He had also agreed to be interviewed at a later date but now he wanted it over with as soon as possible. The thought that his beautiful baby girl would have to have an autopsy sickened him and again the frustration and anger at the situation began to boil up inside. For the first time in his entire life Davey Wiseman was helpless, broken and totally alone. Snatching the handset of the brass telephone that sat on his desk he punched in a number that he now knew off by heart. Giles Barsham was the sub editor of The Sun newspaper and unbeknown to his wife, was a frequent visitor to The Judge's Den. After Davey revealed all that had occurred Giles was chomping at the bit and after approaching one of the senior journalists, the following morning's front page headline had been written in a matter of seconds. It was quickly signed off and Giles Barsham received a pat on the back

from his editor. It was decided that the story was worthy
of the front page as police harassment and wrongful
arrest were current to affairs of the day. It was also felt
that after The Met had been given a chance to reply to the
accusations the paper would be able to run and run with
the story.

The next morning Neil Maddock didn't even get the
chance to take a seat before he was summoned to his
Chief's office only to find Graham Myers was also in
residence.
"What the fuck have you done Neil?"
Graham Myers didn't allow his old friend a chance to
reply and instead launched into a tirade the likes of which
Neil had never been witness to before.
"I fucking told you to leave things alone, in fact I ordered
you to but did you listen? No you did not and you have
arrested a man that will now take The Met to the cleaners
for harassment and wrongful arrest. Fuck me Neil! He's
only just been released on appeal for Christ's sake!"
"But he's guilty Sir, in the light of things maybe not
guilty of the most recent thing I brought him in for but
guilty all the same."
"I don't give a flying fuck if he's a serial killer! Do you
realise what you've done? Don't bother to answer that.
Detective Inspector Maddock I have no other alternative
but to suspend you. You are hereby relieved of duty until
further notice. An internal inquiry will be launched into
your gross misconduct and don't dare to hope that you
will come out of this unscathed because that isn't going
to happen, now clear your desk!"
Neil didn't try to argue, it was obvious he would be
banging his head against a brick wall. The best he could

hope for after twenty five years on the force was that his pension would remain intact. How on earth had it come to this? His word against that of a gangster and he was in no doubt who they were going to believe and it wasn't him. As far as the powers that be were concerned Davey Wiseman could do no wrong or at least that was how it had to appear. In the next twenty four hours it was announced that no charges were being brought and after Gilly and Jimbo had been informed Graham Myers made a personal visit to Davey's home in the hope of talking him out of suing The Metropolitan Police Force. Davey wasn't interested in another court case and he didn't need the money but what the media coverage had given him was leverage and he now had a bargaining tool to find out where Shauna was. Under normal circumstances the Superintendent wouldn't ever entertain doing a deal with a criminal, but desperate times did call for desperate measures and this was most definitely a desperate time. Within the hour Davey had the address of the flat on Rowley Way but he was astute enough to know that he couldn't just turn up there without consequences and having the door slammed in his face was something he would avoid at all costs. Contacting every funeral director in the area, he asked them to inform him if they were instructed to carry out the funeral of a baby girl as he would like to contribute financially as a gift to the mother, in secrecy of course. He was being cautious as the results of the autopsy wouldn't be revealed for a few days but he didn't want to risk missing the date. A small investigation was carried out, which in all honesty amounted to little more than taking statements from those involved. The powers that be informed the coroner that there was no case to answer and a speedy inquest was

183

held after which the verdict on JJ's death was recorded as accidental.

Davey was in the kitchen attempting to prepare some breakfast, which he knew with the best the will in the world he wouldn't be able to eat, when his mobile suddenly burst into life. Snatching it up he heard Gerald Compton introduce himself as the senior partner of Compton and Grange funeral directors. After it was confirmed that the baby was indeed JJ, Davey went on to explain that he would be footing the bill and that the mother was experiencing hard times and as she was a very dear friend Davey wanted to help out financially as a compassionate gesture. He also explained that it was to be a secret and when he said that money was no object Gerald Compton's eyes were suddenly on stalks with greed.

"I must say Sir, that really is a very kind gesture. There shouldn't be too much more of a delay but we will have to wait for the registrars' go-ahead as the poor little might hadn't even been officially recorded as being born."

The man's words hit Davey like a sledgehammer, JJ didn't even have a proper name, well not legally at least and he prayed that Shauna would register him as the father on the birth certificate. It was arranged that Davey would call into the office to make payment once the date and time had been announced. The following day a cheque for ten thousand pounds was handed over and after hearing the meagre items Shauna had ordered which Davey knew could only be down to the lack of funds, the funeral was bumped up to one of the top send offs Compton and Grange had ever organised. A tiny white coffin adorned with pink roses had been chosen along with a white horse drawn hearse and the two snow ponies were to have pink ostrich plumes entwined into their manes. Not once did it cross Davey's mind that this might not have been what Shauna wished for, all he could think of was giving his daughter the best possible send-off not to mention the fact that he wanted the whole world to see that where his child was concerned, there wasn't anything that was too expensive. A plot had already been purchased by Gilly at Carterhatch Lane cemetery and Davey was grateful that Shauna hadn't chosen to have the baby cremated. He wanted somewhere he could visit and a rosebush planted in her memory just wouldn't have cut it but he was surprised that the cemetery was over in Enfield, surprised until he found out that it was a Jewish burial ground. Suddenly all the hatred he'd held onto for a religion he had despised for his entire life disappeared and he was happy that his daughter was to be a part of his past, a part of a family that she had never got to know in life and one that he had stupidly turned his back on. Before the funeral had even taken place he had already planned the headstone and it was going to be a magnificent tribute to the child he had never wanted but who in her short, innocent life, he had come to love and adore.

CHAPTER TWENTY THREE

Awake for most of the night, when the morning of the funeral finally arrived, Davey didn't know what to do with himself. On one hand he wanted the day over with as soon as possible but on the other he never wanted it to end. His mind was in turmoil, he ached to hold Shauna in his arms and knowing that would never happen was tearing him apart.

The service was set for four that afternoon and on entering the small chapel he took a seat at the back and as far out of view as he could. When the solitary pallbearer gently carried JJ's small coffin inside and then walked in the direction of the alter, Davey could feel his fists clench in both anger and heartbreak. Then he saw Shauna slowly walk in and Gilly Slade had his arm around her shoulder making Davey want to rush over and knock him out of the way. He should be the one comforting her, holding her when she cried and there to wipe her tears away, not Gilly. He didn't act on his feelings but when Shauna reached the coffin and threw herself onto it sobbing uncontrollably Davey was forced to place the palm of one hand over his mouth and at the same time wipe away the tears that had begun to fall with the other. Shauna looked so tiny and totally lost, with the little black dress she had borrowed from Gilly's sister-in-law doing absolutely nothing to enhance her looks but then this was no beauty parade, this was a day of nightmares, the likes of which none of them would ever wake up from. How could this have happened? How could their lives have been torn apart in such a small space of time? Deep down he knew the answer, knew that the blame lay squarely at his feet but just how he would ever live with the guilt was another matter. There were no other mourners in attendance and that made Davey feel even sadder, his little girl's life on this mortal coil had been so brief that there were only two people in the whole world that would ever mourn her passing. With the short service concluded the coffin was once again carried outside followed by Shauna and Gilly. Shauna had now composed herself and as she walked down the centre isle she glimpsed Davey. She had known he was the one responsible for the elaborate funeral but she wasn't at all grateful. Why should she be grateful when this was his fault? Every terrible thing that had ever happened in her life was entirely his damn fault. Shauna didn't utter a single word as she passed, she didn't need to as her eyes said it all as they bored so coldly with hatred into his very soul. Gilly on the other hand didn't make eye contact, made no attempt in fact, he simply stared down at the ground as he walked. It wasn't that he was scared, he didn't fear Davey Wiseman, well not on a one to one level at least but today of all days he didn't want any confrontation, any aggro that could possibly make the day worse than it already was. Davey gave it a few minutes before exiting and walking over to the small corner of the graveyard that was set aside specifically for infant deaths, he chose to stand out of the way under a large oak tree as he watched the coffin lowered into the ground.

Before Shauna and Gilly left the graveside, Davey made a discreet exit in the direction of his car. He didn't really have anywhere to go and home was unappealing so heading to The Pelican he hoped that the familiar feeling

187

he usually got as he stepped inside would help in some way, it didn't. Nothing seemed able to lift his spirits and as he walked into his office he wondered if this was how it would be for the rest of his life. Janice had seen him just before he closed the office door and totally unaware of the tragedy that had recently occurred, to her he looked somehow tired and lost. Taking it upon herself to check that he was okay, she knocked and walked in without waiting for an invite. Davey sat with his elbows on the desk, his hands covered his face and for a fleeting moment she actually thought he might be crying. She dismissed the thought immediately, this was Davey Wiseman, The Davey Wiseman, a man feared by most in the criminal world and there was absolutely no way on this earth that he would ever shed a tear over anything.
"You alright boss?"
Davey swiftly turned the swivel chair so that his back was now facing her as he vigorously rubbed at the water running down his cheeks.
"Yeah fine thanks Jan, just a bit tired I expect. Actually I think I'm going to call it a day, is everything okay here?
"Fine. Jimbo's been in and he'll be here again tonight so it's no bother if any of the punters go off on one. You get off home and get some kip, you look done in."

After grabbing a bottle of scotch from the shelf Davey left the club. He had every intention of returning to his apartment but not before he had driven over to Rowley Way. From the shadows he stared up at the flat and could see her standing at the window. It was only a silhouette because of the light burning behind her but he still knew it was her, he also knew that tonight Shauna O'Malley must feel like the loneliest person in the entire

188

world.

That night and for the next few days, Gilly could get little more than just a yes or a no out of Shauna as she spent all of her time just staring out of the window. Linda was fast losing her patience, she felt for the woman, really felt for her but it had been over a week now and she was starting to feel like her home was being treated as a hostel for waifs and strays. Finally when she was near to bursting point she pulled Gilly to one side and was none too compassionate as she made her feelings clear.

"Look love, I know you really like this girl and you're only being kind but it seems that you helping her out is at my expense and to be honest, well it's getting on my fucking nerves if the truth be told. This is my house and I like my routine but lately I feel like I have to tread on fucking egg shells so I don't upset her and it ain't on Gilly."

Gilly didn't want an argument and in all fairness he couldn't blame Linda. She hadn't signed up for any of this and as Shauna wasn't the easiest person to be around at the moment, maybe it would be better if they left and found somewhere else to stay. It wasn't as if he didn't have any money and after all that had happened, well Davey owed her big time, so dipping into the cash now didn't feel so wrong.

"I totally understand sweetheart, you've been great to both of us and I won't forget that in a hurry. First thing tomorrow I'll look for somewhere else okay?"

Linda smiled and then gave him a peck on the check. Grabbing her coat she decided to have a snout down Camden Market. It was full of tourists but there was just something about the place, the noise, the music blearing

189

out and the smell of the foreign food stalls that always made her feel good.

Gilly sat alone in the front room and the ticking of the mantle clock soon began to irritate him. Sighing heavily he reasoned that he might as well start having a look about today, what was the point of waiting until tomorrow when he knew that finding accommodation, well at least anything that was half decent, was hard enough as it was without leaving it until the last minute. Poking his head around the door he saw her standing in her usual place just staring vacantly out at the world.

"I have to pop out sweetheart, you going to be alright?"

For the first time since the funeral she suddenly engaged in conversation and it warmed his heart.

"Fine. Gilly can I please ask you a favour?"

"Sure darlin', you can ask me anything you like."

"Will you promise me that you will never again have any contact with Jacks? I don't want her to know about...."

Shauna paused for a moment and he could see the tears forming in her eyes and hear the quaver in her voice when she eventually began to speak again.

"I don't ever want her to know about JJ, it would kill her."

"I promise babe, now why don't you try and get some rest?"

Shauna nodded her head but rest was the last thing on her mind. Over the past few days she hadn't just been staring out of the window for no good reason, Shauna had been watching people come and go and it hadn't taken her long to see a pattern, a pattern that was going to give her what she wanted. Waiting a few minutes until she was sure Gilly wouldn't return she reached into her pocket and pulled out a bundle of notes, it was the all the money she'd had on her the day she left Jackie's. Stepping from the flat she placed the door onto the latch and then made her way downstairs to the iconic walkway that is The Rowley Way. Alexandru Dalcu hadn't yet reached his twentieth birthday but had been selling drugs since his arrival from Romania two years earlier. He was an illegal immigrant but with friends already living in London he had gone under the radar and hadn't experienced any trouble with immigration. Alexandru knew it was risky making his living this way but it was also the easiest and most profitable. He'd been advised to go to the Home Counties for land work but it had never appealed to him and besides, why the fuck should he do all the shitty hard work that the Brits were too lazy to undertake? Alexandru had dreams, big dreams and as soon as he'd made enough money he was getting out of this toilet of a country and heading for warmer shores. Shauna had been observing him every day and now knew his movements off by heart, for a drug dealer he wasn't that clever, even she knew that you shouldn't be regimented just in case the police were watching. As she approached him Alexandru smiled at the pretty dark haired woman. Admittedly she was a fair few years older than him but still very attractive and if it was offered he wouldn't have turned her down. He expected her to walk on by but when she stopped dead in front of him he gave her a quizzical look.

"Do you have any smack?"

Alexandru almost choked in shock and then began to laugh. His English was pretty good but he still had a strong accent and Shauna had to listen hard to understand him.

"You having a laugh with me lady?"

"No I'm deadly serious, I have money."

For a brief moment Alexandru studied Shauna wondering if she was the Law but something in her eyes, a deep, deep sadness told him 'no', she was just struggling to get through this shit hole they all had the misfortune to call life.

"You ever used before?"

"No. Just say if that's going to stop you selling to me, because there are plenty of others that will be only too happy. Look kid, I'm not asking to be your friend, I just want to purchase some stuff, so are you going to sell it to me or not?"

Alexandru removed a wrap from his pocket and passed it over.

"That's a tenner."

"Not so fast sunshine, I want two and a stick as well."

Shauna remembered the terminology from her childhood, how could she ever forget it? Suddenly everything from her early years flooded back with blinding clarity.

"If you ain't never used before then even one is too much, maybe try a half a wrap and save the rest for later?"

Shauna pulled out the notes from her pocket and from then on the dealer lost all concern for the woman's welfare and after swiftly passing over the second wrap, proceeded to take out a syringe from his top pocket.

Shauna paid the going rate and as Alexandru handed over his wares he held onto her hand for a second longer than was necessary.

"Take it easy babe, nothing's worth what you're about to do."

"I haven't got a clue what you're on about."

Shauna turned to walk away but Alexandru couldn't

resist one last attempt.

"Lady I've seen the exact same look that you have in your eyes a thousand times before. I also know that if you're hell bent on going to that place, then there's nothing I or anyone else can say or do to stop you." Shauna only nodded her head and after giving the young man a thin weak attempt at a smile, she made her way up to the flat as quickly as she could. Alexandru knew that there would be no repeat sales from the woman in the future and with a bad feeling he decided to call it a day, business had been slow and if this strange woman had been able to spot him so easily then the Old Bill would have no trouble. In the past it had never bothered him in the slightest who he sold to, if the idiots were stupid enough to want his wares then who was he to argue but something about his last sale was playing on his mind. It might have been that he was just plain tired of all the bullshit but whatever it was that was bothering Alexandru, it was making him feel really bad. Maybe it was simply time to move patch, even a change of career to pastures new didn't now seem like such a bad idea.

Gilly's little trip out had started off slowly and after calling in at several Estate Agents he was beginning to wonder if he would ever find a place. Picking up a copy of The Camden New Journal he took a seat at a table outside Heaven Canal Café. It was one of those veggie places which he wasn't really that keen on but he couldn't deny that they really knew how to make a decent cup of coffee. Scanning the small advertisements at the back of the newspaper he removed his mobile and began to make calls. With each knock back he circled the advert with a pen and when he'd reached the final few,

193

which were only advertising bedsits and definitely not suitable for himself and Shauna, he slammed the paper down onto the table. Gilly heard a discreet cough and then a male voice say 'excuse me. Glancing up he met the gaze of a rather bohemian looking gentleman who must have been in his early seventies at least.

"I don't mean to pry but from the look of that newspaper and what you've done to it I would maybe hazard a guess that you're perhaps looking for some accommodation?"

"Yeah but I think looking is about as far as I'm gonna get today, every single place, well at least anything that's half decent, has already been snapped up."

"Then this might just be your lucky day young man. I have a friend who is looking for a new tenant, the last lot upped and left owing him a month's rent. I think he'd prefer not to let out his basement again but he has a mortgage to pay and needs must I suppose. Would you like me to give him a call?"

Gilly wasn't about to look a gift horse in the mouth and after all, having a look wasn't going to cost him anything even if the place turned out to be a complete khazi.

CHAPTER TWENTY FOUR

With the front door firmly closed behind her Shauna set about finding something to use as a tourniquet. The only thing remotely suitable was Linda's hairdryer and after wrapping the power cord tightly around her upper arm, she tucked a wooden spoon between the cord and her skin and began to slowly turn. It nipped like mad and she winced but nothing was going to stop her. When she was happy that a vein in her arm was sufficiently pumped she began to carry out the ritual of cooking up the heroin on one of Linda's old desert spoons. It was a ritual Shauna had seen her own mother carry out so many times and back then it had scared her but not now, not now that her mind was made up. As soon as the dirty brown powder turned to a golden liquid Shauna steadied her hand before siphoning up every last drop from the spoon. She wasn't prepared to take any chances and had used, against Alexandru's advice, both wraps. Shauna slowly positioned her arm and began to inject. In a matter of seconds she felt a mind blowing rush as the heroin sped through her veins and mixed with her blood. Her last image was of Vonny and JJ before she slipped into a self-imposed stupor, one from which she would never ever awake.

Gilly felt really pleased with himself, like a cat that had got the cream and couldn't wait to get back to Shauna and share the good news. Thanks to a chance meeting, he had managed to secure a nice little flat over in Wimbledon on a six month lease. It was in a lovely quiet area and far enough from Davey Wiseman or at least that's what he hoped for. Placing his key into the lock he called out as he opened the front door and stepped into the hall. There was no answer and he guessed she must have gone for a lie down. Pie and mash was in order tonight and he knew that Linda would be pleased she didn't have to cook but also pleased to celebrate the fact that she would soon be getting the place all to herself again. Tapping lightly on the bedroom door Gilly turned the handle as quietly as he could then tiptoed inside. The sight that greeted him stopped him dead in his tracks. Shauna, though slightly slumped forwards, was still in a seated position. Her head was bowed low with the syringe still inserted into her arm.

"No, no, no!!!!!!"

Running over he lifted her head to face him but there was no response. He felt for a pulse but there was nothing and her skin was cold and clammy to the touch.

"Don't you dare fucking do this to me now, why, why, why baby, why have you done this? We could have got through all the pain, it might have taken a long time but I know we could have, oh Shauna, I love you so much darlin' please don't leave me."

Cradling her head to his chest he began to sob uncontrollably and the tears were still falling ten minutes later when Linda got home from the market.

"I'm back, anyone fancy putting the kettle on?"

The bedroom door was wide open and as she stepped into the room she was speechless at the scene she found. Her silence only lasted for a second or two.

"What the fuck!"

Gilly didn't say a word as Linda rushed over.

"Move out of the way Gilly, let me have a look."

Gilly stayed exactly where he was, still clutching Shauna to him.

"I said, move out of the fucking way!"

Linda Slade had to prise her brother-in-law's fingers open and then pushed him to the side. Finally he let go of Shauna completely and Linda instantly knew that here was no saving the woman. Pulling out her mobile phone she tapped in nine nine nine and shook her head as she impatiently waited for her call to be answered by the emergency services. The ambulance was there in a matter of minutes and as it was an unexplained death, a detective and uniformed police officer arrived soon after. The paramedics made a full examination and it was clear that there was no hope of resuscitation as the woman had been dead for quite a while.

That day Shauna O'Malley was declared deceased at two forty four pm. The police had entered the flat through the open door and for a second it struck Linda that it was the first time the Old Bill had crossed over her threshold when they hadn't been after either her ex-husband or her brother-in-law. After being brought up to speed by the paramedics Detective Owen Peters asked Linda and Gilly a few questions but spying the syringe and other drug paraphernalia he knew there was no foul play, it was purely accidental, just another druggie overdose. Owen instructed the PC to close his notebook and after a polite goodbye to Linda, the two men let themselves out of the flat. Linda tried to comfort Gilly when he once again began to cry but what she said came out bluntly and all wrong.

"Whatever got into her stupid head, the leery little cow!"

Gilly sharply pulled away from her embrace and stood bolt upright. His face was contorted with such anger that Linda knew if looks could kill she would have been dead

197

several times over.

"Her baby died, she's been held prisoner in filthy conditions, not to mention a whole other fucking bunch of shit that neither you nor I would have been able to cope with, so what do you expect?"

"I'm sorry I didn't........"

"It's a bit late for that! Just think before you fucking speak in future Linda."

Storming from the flat Gilly was consumed with rage, rage that Shauna was gone, rage that she had felt she had no other choice but to take her own life and rage that Davey was still alive. He was the one to blame for all of this and once again he was getting off scot free. With that thought Gilly started to run, he ran like never before, like nothing on earth would be able to stop him and just over thirty minutes later he came to a halt outside Davey's apartment building. Panting heavily he allowed himself a moment to compose himself and get his breath back and then reaching into his pocket he removed the key fob. Entering through the main door, this time he didn't care who saw him, didn't care if his image was recorded by the close circuit cameras and pressing for the lift, he made his way up to the penthouse.

Davey had been home all day making plans, desperately trying to work out how he could console her, make her love him again. He heard the gentle whir of the lift shaft but thought nothing of it as it was a constant noise throughout the day when other residents came and went. When his front door suddenly burst open and Gilly Slade entered the flat he was momentarily stunned. His eyes narrowed in anger as he stepped forward.

"You've got some fucking nerve!"

"You cunt!!!!!"

Davey didn't have a chance to reply as Gilly ran across the room and launched himself knocking Davey to the ground. The two men wrestled but Gilly was so enraged and had a force far superior to his usual strength, that for once he had the upper hand.

"She's dead, she's fucking dead and it's all because of you, you cunt!"

His words stunned Davey and as Gilly straddled him and reigned down blow after blow Davey offered no resistance. Blood flowed from his nose and mouth but suddenly and as swiftly as the attack had begun, it ended. Gilly got to his feet and for reasons known only to himself he held out his hand and helped Davey to get up. After wiping the blood with the sleeve of his shirt Davey just stared at Gilly in total bewilderment, partly down to shock but mostly down to the disbelief that the man actually had the balls to walk into his apartment and attack him.

"I know you're both reeling over the baby's death but fuck me Gilly, I had no hand in that."

"I don't mean JJ you tosser, Shauna!!!!!"

The words hit Davey like a sledge hammer and dropping to his knees he began to howl wildly. The pain he felt was like nothing he could ever have imagined and as the tears and snot flowed he didn't care who saw him, didn't care that he was Davey Wiseman hard man and gangster. Right at this moment in time he felt as though his heart had been ripped out. This was so different from before, there would never be a chance to say 'I'm sorry', never be a chance to try and put things right. She was gone from his life and he could never hold her in his arms again and tell her that he loved her.

199

"When? How? Oh fuck no, tell me it ain't so please!!!!!!!"

"She took heroin just like her mother, only she knew exactly what she was doing, no one turned her into a junkie, she just wanted out of this nightmare. I guess in her mind she always felt that she had to make you pay and by fuck she's done that."

"But I could have got her some help with the grief, made things right I know I could."

Gilly slowly shook his head and then smirked in a disgusted manner. With a heavy heart he turned and walked towards the front door but before he pulled it open and disappeared out of Davey's life forever, he had a few final words that would play on the gangster's mind until the day he died.

"You are a truly sad, pathetic cunt Davey Wiseman and a sorry excuse for a human being but I know deep down that you loved her, we both did but you are the one who will have her death on your conscience for the rest of your life. I suppose when it boils down to it and in a sad kind of way, Shauna O'Malley finally settled the score and paid you back!"

As the lift door closed Gilly inhaled deeply. When he heard the howling and sobbing begin all over again from the apartment it brought him no comfort at all, how could it when he too felt so totally dead inside?

THE END

Printed in Great Britain
by Amazon